Number 10

6.

Number 10

Richard Ingrams and John Wells

Illustrated by Brian Bagnall

PRIVATE EYE/ANDRE DEUTSCH

Published in Great Britain by Private Eye Productions Ltd,
6 Carlisle Street, London W1
in association with
André Deutsch Ltd, 105-106 Great Russell Street, London W1

© 1989 Pressdram Ltd
Illustrations by Brian Bagnall © 1989

ISBN 233 98477 1

Printed by The Bath Press, Bath, Avon

HOTEL TRUDEAU
   SHULMAN AVENUE
      TORONTO
                                   24 JUNE 1988

Dear Bill,
Maurice has managed to get a pair for the Centre Court on Saturday week, street value £1500 a piece, but they were a little gesture of gratitude after I managed to ease the way for his housing estate down in Sussex. Brother Ridley takes a very sensible line on that sort of thing and feels, like me, that there are far too many restrictions on the development of arable land in so-called areas of outstanding natural beauty, when everybody knows we produce too much food as it is. He got a lot of stick last week because he once put a stop to some spiv knocking up eyesores in his back garden, but he has no objection to that sort of thing in principle. Rather a lah-de-dah fellow, but basically one of us, and Maurice Picarda adores him.

I'm writing this in the Boeing on the way to somewhere in Canada. Nicely is snoring at my side, having consumed not only his First Class In-Flight Tour d'Argent Executive Lunch but also my own. I can't eat that kind of muck any more, so Boris makes me up a crate and a packet of crisps.

I was quite glad to get the Boss airborne, as her bloomers have been in something of a tangle all week, what with the Irish beak deliberately flouting her will and refusing to hand over the wanted gunman, and of course our young soccer ambassadors in Dusseldorf. Poor Hurd, pretty crestfallen after his failed leadership bid, was whistled round the moment the papers arrived. 'You've got to do something, Douglas,' I heard her stentorian bellow before he'd had time to button his cardigan, 'you're the Home Secretary. Law and Order is your responsibility. These young thugs are sending entirely the wrong signals to our friends in Europe. We are the economic leaders, an enterprise society based on a firm moral ethic, as you yourself have said, following my lead. I have arranged for a microphone to be put out on the pavement, and the gentlemen of the Press are already assembled to hear your six-point plan for dealing with this blot on our image.'

Hurd hummed and ha-ed, saying he needed time to consult his department, but M. would hear none of it and took him by the scruff to thrust him out of the front door where he was

'... Nicely is snoring at my side...'

duly devoured by the waiting crocodiles. Now the little greaser has come up with a few damnfool ideas to placate the Boss, most absurd of which is a round the clock ban on the consumption of alcohol in a public place, as if that's got anything to do with it. Next thing we know, you and I will be cracking a few miniatures in the rough, when Hurd's Prohibition Squad will come thundering over the horizon and clap us in irons before you can say Electric Soup.

The only comfort to Margaret was poor little Ginger Nuts Kinnock drifting even further up shit creek and not a paddle in sight. As if the mad tea-drinker was not enough, one of the few normal human beings in his team, Denzil Davies, a fellow Welshman of very sound views on the Bomb etcetera and like all his tribe no mean hammerer of the optics, is dozing over the TV one day and is jerked awake by the sight of Pillock announcing on the spur of the moment that he's changed his mind and decided not to ban the bomb after all. Having had the rug well and truly pulled out from under his feet, our Taffy goes out on a bender with some goggle-eyed reptile he was at school with, and, egged on by his portly friend, becomes very steamed up about wild impulsive leaks to the media by Brer Kinnock. He then rings up the Press Association in the middle of the night to announce his resignation. Having been on the verge of doing exactly the same thing in the wee small hours on many occasions I felt a good deal of sympathy for him, about not being consulted etc.

I'll give you a bell when I get back from the Land of the Moose, and we'll fix up a foursome at Lamberhurst. Furniss has promised Maurice he'll toddle down to talk about further developments for PicHomes at Scotney.

Lawson's head has now fallen in my lap so I must close. Have a really nice day.

There you go,

DENIS

10 Downing Street
Whitehall

8 JULY 1988

Dear Bill,

Poor little Pillock, as you will have observed in the *Telegraph*, has been very much on the ropes over the last few days and spitting teeth. According to Boris it all started when he had two lagers in the hospitality room at the BBC before a programme called 'This Year Next Year' and tore off his CND badge in front of the viewers. Needless to say when he got home it was Cold Tongue Pie for supper, Glenys being a paid-up member of the Greenham Common Troop, and next morning the big union Johnnies were on the blower threatening to withdraw their funds.

Poor Ginger Nuts, by now stone cold sober, thereupon invited himself to breakfast at that newspaper Maurice's stepson works for, and held forth for the best part of two hours over the croissants and freshly made coffee to the effect that he had in no way changed his mind, and that his view had always been whatever it was he had said before and not what people might have said it was after.

All this was obediently printed verbatim over several pages by the bespectacled egg in charge, and Pillock's rating shot down to the Lower Ground Floor. Naturally our rank and file at Halitosis Hall went apeshit, throwing their waistcoats in the air and howling with delight at the little bald fellow's discomfiture. It all got to such a pitch that some then had to be restrained from playing spudarse up and down the corridors and peeing in the Thames. This inevitably reached the ears of little Tinker Bell, M's marketing man, and an order went out pronto to cool it, the thinking at HQ being that once Pillock was off the end of the plank and into the shark-infested waters, they could bring in some person of normal intelligence, like this Smith man, and we'd all be in trouble.

You may remember the similar situation at Burmah some years back when there was a move to oust that old wino Managing Director with the pebble glasses – Hotchkiss, Connolly? no matter. We all used to cheer him to the echo at

'... and tore off his CND badge in front of the viewers ...'

the AGM in case they put in somebody who'd start cracking down on the Exes.

Talking of replacements, I think Mogadon may be following poor old Whitelaw into the bed next to the door. He was already in bad odour for supporting Nicely in the Battle of the Interest Rates, when up he pops, eyes wide open and without having touched a drop, and tells the hacks to forget all about the Boss, he invented Thatcherism, had his arm up her back all the time making her mouth work. The Boss was predictably fit to be tied, and said the next time they went to Brussels together Howe could go Tourist with all his evil-smelling civil servants.

Baker, that one with the Brilliantine hairdo and the American specs, has also been getting the rough end of her tongue. She rings him up shortly after midnight and two hours before breakfast regular as clockwork to demand higher standards in the Classroom. I happened to be standing by the phone the other evening filling my hot water bottle with Electric Soup as he was getting the gamma rays down the wire, and it sounded to me at one point as though he'd finally blown his top. 'Don't talk to me like that, Kenneth,' Margaret scolded, 'I was at Education when you were still in nappies. If it wasn't for me you'd still be working in Harrods' shirt department. No, it is not preposterous. And how many of your schoolchildren could spell that word, I wonder? I shall expect an answer on my desk by seven tomorrow morning. Goodbye.' With that she hung up, giving me a look as if to question why I needed a hot water bottle in July, and shot off into the den to do her boxes.

Boris himself is very upset about Glasnost. According to him, all the Russian yobs have got the bit between their teeth and think they can jump up and down at the equivalent of the Tory Party Annual Conference demanding potatoes and other luxuries, when in the old days they'd have known damn well that kind of lark would mean twenty years in the Gulag, and a very good thing too, according to Boris. His view is that Gorbo is all piss and wind anyway, but he's worried about his concessionary rates at hotels on the Black Sea and the annual ration of free caviar he gets for being a member of the Party.

Sorry I missed you at Wimbledon. I ran into that man with the moustache and the wooden leg who used to run Accounts at Atlas Preservatives, who'd brought supplies with him in the back of the Alvis, so we both got legless together and I finished by being driven home by Tebbit's bodyguard.

Yours still recovering from the Mixed Doubles,

DENIS

10 Downing Street
Whitehall

22 JULY 1988

Dear Bill,
You were quite right to telephone the other night about Pillock in Coonland. Did you see his Meakers' Tropicana flared trouser suit with matching shades? Squiffy and I laughed for hours in the Club. What a prize arsehole he is! I had a letter only today from Mrs Van der Kafferbesher, saying that he had been going round all the various front line states, slagging the

Boss in front of ordinary Africans in the street, and generally egging on Oliver Rambo. As she pointed out, there is a code, i.e. that you don't abuse the family in front of strangers, and in this case it can only damage the standing of Big White Brother down there with regard to future exports of fancy goods, paint strippers etc.

Mrs Van der K. dwells at length in her letter on Ginger Nuts' physical appearance, and then continues: 'My friend in our secret police, Colonel Joost Niejurker, has told us in confidence that Mr and Mrs Kinnock were both guests in Harare at the table of the Marxist dictator Kenneth Kaunda. According to the tapes, Mr Kinnock rose visibly swaying and said he wasn't used to these high temperatures. (A likely story, dear Denis, but you know these Communists never have very strong heads for drink. You remember George Brown.) Well then, would you believe this? He began by making dubious jokes about your respected Chancellor, Mr Nigel Lawson. Well, of course, all the Sambos fell about, rolling their eyes and slapping their pink hands together. It is easy enough to make them laugh. You remember Dorcas, our daily, now very irritatingly in detention, she was always weeping with laughter. I only had to open my mouth for her to be off in peals. However, this does not excuse Mr Kinnock, who went on − I hope you will forgive me for mentioning this, Denis − about yourself, which wounded us all deeply. I would not have drawn it to your attention, but I think you should know that the Marxist Kinnock, egged on by his chippy little CND wife, had the barefaced cheek, Denis, to outline a scenario in which you were dying. One of your friends, he pretended, asked what your last words were, to which the reply came: "He did not have any, his wife was with him to the end." This was suggesting, Denis, that your dear Margaret is so insensitive to her fellow human beings, that she would continue to talk despite the fact that her beloved dear one was at that moment passing over into Abraham's Bosom. Can you imagine a more derogatory and offensive suggestion to make? But of course his audience of Oxford-trained Communists shrieked with laughter and wiped their eyes with their silk handkerchiefs, just like the monkeys in the zoo. As I said to Groet, "Let him try coming here, and telling that brand of tasteless humour!" But of course, like all these revolutionaries he is a coward, and does not set foot on our soil.'

'. . . to do a song and dance act for that cheeky little leprechaun in the wig . . .'

Sound stuff, I think you will agree. Fortunately, we had the last laugh, when Mr and Mrs Pillock were mistaken for South African tourists and clapped in the nick by a bunch of trigger-happy Tons-Tons.

You ask me the latest on Mogadon Man. Boss got very miffed the other night: Mogadon was on his feet at Halitosis Hall, holding forth on some cause dear to his heart when he suddenly looked at his watch, shoved his speech into his pocket, bowed to the Speaker muttering about having to be in another place, and buggered off. Gradually it got round that he hadn't gone to the House of Lords at all, but that a big car had been waiting to take him out to the TV centre at Shepherds Bush to do a song and dance act for that cheeky little leprechaun in the wig. He got back to the debate an hour or so later, still in make-up, and everybody hooted. The official line is that this Wogan act was all part of his demon plan to nobble the Boss. Boris on the other hand thinks he's probably in love.

You may have seen that Smarmy Cecil has been given another leg-up by Margaret as her revenge on Mr Nicely next door at Number 11. Cecil couldn't wait to tell me the news himself, and came oiling up at drinks for Mr Izal Ataturk the other night, saying he was now in charge of the Star Chamber, with power to veto all Nigel's decisions. Fatso is always just as rude to him as he is to me, asking him where his suits come from and if he wants the name of a good stockbroker, so he really has no one to blame but himself.

I ran into Maurice at Lytham St Anne's, in a sorry state. The Air Malta lady has gone into a very expensive clinic to have her face lifted, and Ronald Ferguson is making his life intolerable at the Club with his complaints about the in-laws. See you at Gatwick. I've been on to the Major's son-in-law who runs the Duty Free at the Village and he says we can have the VIP lounge to ourselves for the day or until such time as we take off, whichever is longer.

Hasta la Costa,

DENIS

DENMARG
   CONSTANTINE BAY
   PADSTOW
      CORNWALL

19 AUGUST 1988

Dear Bill,

I trust you got my p.c. from Bangkok and that Daphne did not see fit to confiscate it. Maurice had very kindly provided me with a long list of names and addresses passed on to him by some funny old literary johnny he met on the Inter-city to Taunton. If you see him you might say that regrettably I was not allowed off the leash at any stage and our Siamese sight-seeing was confined to visiting the Buddhist temples (when you've seen one you've seen them all).

I insisted on a week of R & R here following our final touchdown at Heathrow, such was my state of mental confusion after two weeks of remorseless globe-trotting. Needless to say the Boss was on a high throughout, though even she, if you ask me, is beginning to find that kind of schedule a bit too much of a good thing. She was pretty pissed off by the behaviour of the Ozzies; though, after our experiences with those Qantas people in the Algarve who tried to set fire to Mother Flack's thatched parasols, I had warned her that the days in which respectful colonials turn out to doff their caps to the Great White Mother were very much a thing of the past. She might have recalled the treatment accorded to her emissary Sir Robert Armstrong who was sent out to put the fear of God into them over the Wright book only to be told in no uncertain terms by some senior legal luminaries to go and put his head up a dead bear's bum. However as she doesn't get much chance nowadays of pressing the flesh with the *hoi polloi* on her home ground she would insist on doing her Royal walkabout act in the middle of Sydney which, as you well know, has long since ceased to be the Tunbridge Wells of the S. Hemisphere and is nowadays a breeding ground for all kinds of weirdos, Trotskyists, AIDS-infected poofters and other riff-raff. As soon as the Boss switched on her smile and waded into the crowd we were engulfed by a mass of evil-smelling Commies all shouting the odds on behalf of the IRA. No security of any kind and I distinctly heard one top rank policeman remarking to his colleague that the 'spooky old bat' (i.e. the Boss) had only herself to blame. Worse was to come – she went off to the local TV studio to go six rounds with their equivalent of the piss-artist in the bow-tie Sir Robin Thingy, expecting it to be a doddle, instead of which the inquisitor turns out to be another pinko rough-neck totally lacking in any of the common courtesies. When he insisted on the Boss answering his question about South African sanctions she quite rightly to my mind ripped off the microphone and stormed out of the studio saying she had to be at the hairdresser's.

After that it all became a bit of a haze. I can't remember whether we went to India, but it was somewhere very hot with a whole lot of spindly folk shuffling about in loin-cloths. Then for some reason the Boss insisted on hiring a helicopter to the Gulf and paying a call on the gallant tars of the Armadillo patrol. We scrambled out on the deck of HMS *Fergie* to find a bunch of pretty dazed-looking sea-dogs wondering what the hell was going on. The Boss then marched into the Captain's cabin, seized the microphone and gave them all a little pep-talk over the intercom telling them that every single person in the UK was very proud of what they were doing 'over and out'.

As I write she is sitting in her deck chair working out her

'... bossy-boots Currie who was jogging along the N. Yorks coastal path ...'

new blueprint to bring about the social regeneration of Britain and instil a new sense of moral responsibility into the layabouts and soccer hooligans. This is all to get the better of Hurd who has been making a desperate attempt of late to wrest the moral high ground from her control. I am about to leave her to it and stagger up to the green where I have a date with the Major's brother-in-law and his accountant friend Pringle, the one who was drummed out of the Rotary for pissing in the window-box during the Grand Master's speech. A very merry soul, albeit clearly in need of a spot of social regeneration – but then you could say the same for all of us.

By the by, you probably saw that she brought in that fatty-puff Kenneth Clarke to give a new caring image at the Min. of Health. (Also little Mellor was transferred to the same dept. after he'd offended some party big-wigs by shooting his mouth off once too often on the West Bank.) Well, when this latest Nurses' pay crisis blew up it turned out that the new team was so laid-back that every single one of them was on holiday – including bossy-boots Currie who was jogging along the N. Yorks coastal path in a silly track-suit. The Boss was absolutely livid and rang round everyone saying how dare they take a summer holiday, that she had always managed perfectly well without one and that it was only her consideration for the needs of weaker and older brethren (i.e. yours truly) which forced her from time to time to absent herself from her desk.

Yours cretinously,

DENIS

10 Downing Street
Whitehall

2 SEPTEMBER 1988

Dear Bill,

I hope I wasn't *de trop* at your soiree with your niece last Thursday, but as I said I am not accustomed to being in London in August and seeing the lights on in the Athenaeum Massage and Sports Club, I couldn't resist dropping in for a quick one. Had you not been obliged to leave so soon in order to take your niece to the station I would have explained how I came to be back in town.

The scenario was two weeks R & R in Cornwall, the location chosen by Tinker Bell, Margaret's image maker, for its proximity to the golf course, enhancing the Boss's profile as the devoted spouse, sacrificing her career for a loved one. I refrained from pointing out that if golf was the name of the game I'd far rather be hammering the optics with Mother Flack.

Of course, as you would expect, 'Denmarg' was transformed from a dampish detached res. (three bed with sea views suit retired couple) into a fortress, telephones ringing night and day, eight secretaries at work in the garage, and a posse of SAS men patrolling in the rhododendrons. Except for one photocall on the first green I was not allowed out of the house, and was confined to a smallish pantry with a view of the back wall, where Boris was decent enough to bring me supplies on his bike from the Off-Licence in Padstow. Margaret appeared every afternoon at four-thirty, saying 'This is all for your benefit, Denis. You know this is the kind of holiday you like, a quiet English affair away from the hustle and bustle.'

'. . . Boris was decent enough to bring me supplies on his bike from the Off-Licence . . .'

So you can imagine the relief when the red phone rang in the early hours to report some new beastliness among the Bogtrotters. I heard the Boss through the wall as she hit the floor for a Scramble, and within minutes the caravanserai was revving up on the gravel to return to Downing Street. I pleaded in vain from an upper window that I would be in the way only to be told that it was a time of national crisis – come downstairs in my dressing gown – I could dress in the back of the typing van.

We then had the usual farce of poor little Tom King being summoned over and shouted at for several hours. Even from my snug in the attic I couldn't help hearing the tone of shrill insistence. 'These are evil men. They must be wiped off the face of the world! We know who they are, we have their telephone numbers, why are they not behind barbed wire?' I heard poor King muttering his traditional rubric about it not being quite as simple as that, Prime Minister, only to be silenced by an imperious roar. Then the front door flew open, and I saw the crumpled-suited figure reel across the road to where a huge battery of cameras and microphones had been set up to record his assurances that something was even then being done, but that it would be playing into the enemy's hands to reveal anything at this stage. He then wheeled smartly about and returned to the house for another session of GBH.

You probably remember the same routine over the Hooligans when Hurd and that little tiny one whose name nobody ever knows were driven out to do a double act on the doorstep. It put me very much in mind of Prosser-Cluff's Christmas panto in K.L. when the old boy was playing Widow Twankey and had imbibed a little too heavily to steady his nerves. His ADC – Phelps? Wapshott? no matter – was constantly forced on to the stage by an unseen hand to reassure the audience that any delay was due to a fault in the slide projector.

Not content with lashing the wretched King, Margaret was also determined to sabotage Fatso's American Express Seventeen Great Restaurants in Four Days Tour in the Land of the Frogs. When the figures came in from the Bank of England it became clear that Matey's chickens had come home to roost, and that this time not even his fanclub on the back benches could save him from the wrath to come. I had the good fortune to see the family party as they arrived back, hot and dusty, with their little brood loudly complaining in the back of the car. 'Ah Nigel!' I cried, 'I wasn't expecting to see you back till next week. I hope nothing is wrong?' He contented himself with a Churchillian gesture of defiance, but I could see that my bon mot had found its mark.

Within the hour, Matey had changed out of his wine-stained shorts and 'I ate the world' T-shirt, and bowled in spruce and suited to face the music. 'No, no, I do not mind being disturbed in the middle of the night,' he began as she swept before him into the Sanctum and slammed the door, 'and I am always ready to listen to the views of Professor Walters, even at three o'clock in the morning, but I do assure you that there is absolutely no cause whatsoever for any alarm. A further fine tuning of interest rates . . .' 'Ha!' Margaret cut in, 'that is the eighth time you have said that, Nigel, and look what good it has done. The spending boom is out of control, and it is all your fault for cutting taxes in that disastrous Budget of yours.' A few hours in the sun seemed to have strengthened the resolve of our portly friend. 'With respect, Prime Minister,' I heard him continue, 'if you recall, the policy of lightening the tax burden, particularly on wealth creators, has all along been your personal priority. I seem to remember you described my Budget, notwithstanding a certain froideur that then existed between us, as "positively brilliant". Correct me if I am wrong. However, if you do not like what is happening, I shall be more than ready to surrender my portfolio. No doubt you have considered your friend Cecil. I believe he has a brilliant head for figures.' With this I heard the squeak of rubber on marble as he spun on his heel and left the room. Clearly anticipating the Prosser-Cluff gambit on the doorstep, he then left the house by the garden door and shinned over the wall.

Would you like to come down to the launch of Maurice's PicRail Consortium at Dover which is mounting a bid to run private trains on the existing Southern Region network? He asked me to get Channon to come, but he's always rather snooty when I ask him to things, and I think it would be more productive to treat it as a megafreebie and book ourselves into some motel within reeling distance.

Yours in the Executive Buffet,

DENIS

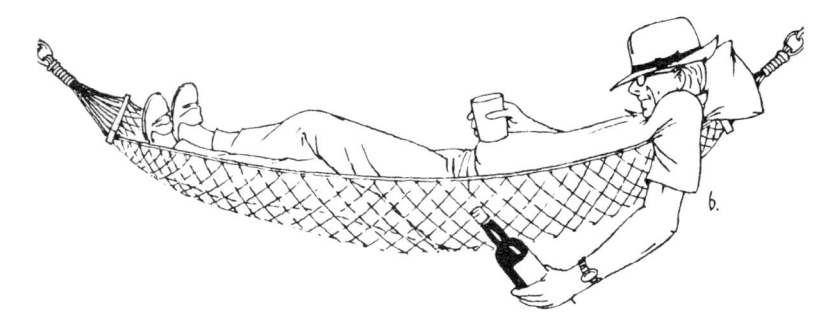

10 Downing Street
Whitehall

16 SEPTEMBER 1988

Dear Bill,

Thank you for your congratulatory card showing the old gentleman with the ear trumpet and the caption 'Another Old Grandad if you please'. Boris explained that it contained some reference to alcohol, and I'm sure you and the Major found it very amusing. One of Maurice's PicMail Greased Lightning Couriers brought it round on a skateboard, demanding a ten-pound surcharge.

I must say I have mixed feelings about the forthcoming happy event in Texas. Boss is over the moon about the continuation of the Thatcher line and hopes it's a girl who will be ready to take over as MT the Second by the time she feels like handing in her pail. But anything springing out of the loins of the Boy Mark and through the Burgerdorfer genes strikes me as likely to be pretty repellent. Don't say I said that or it'll be cold tongue pie again from now to Christmas.

Aren't you pretty cross about this Gib business? The Boss was fit to be tied when she was told that an inquest was going to be held, and threatened to give the Rock back to Spain immediately. After a great deal of toing and froing, however, little Howe managed to get it put off until the Summer Recess, thus preventing the Smellysocks from making too much capital out of it at Halitosis Hall. Now, would you believe, they're kitting the SAS out in various comic opera costumes, false moustaches, dark glasses etc. and putting them behind a screen from which they give their evidence in a parade ground roar that makes the Coroner's dentures rattle. Anyone can tell it's all a load of codswallop about the Paddies being in satellite communication with General Gadaffi, able to call down a nuclear strike at any moment. What I can't understand is why they don't tell Señor Pizzaparlor the truth, i.e. that they'd identified three wanted terrorists and got a memo from the Boss to rub them out pronto *pour encourager les autres*. I thought the *Sun* put it very well with that big headline saying 'Plug 'em full o' holes!' I don't think people realise how sound the Boss is on the IRA.

'... behind a screen from which they give their evidence in a parade ground roar...'

Talking of security, would you believe that our lot are spending a cool mill on debugging the Grand so that we can make our triumphal return there next month for the Conference? Whole streets are being dug up for miles around, the sea off Brighton will be depth-charged as a precaution against Libyan submarines, and both piers occupied by the military to forestall a Cherbourg-style landing by the Provos. All this to demonstrate clearly to the West that we are not being intimidated by the men of violence.

Poor little Pillock didn't fare too well on his Awayday to Bournemouth. The new autumn collection from Transport House is apparently targeting Caring Yuppies, and the

Brothers didn't take too kindly to it. When Pillock appealed to them to collaborate with the Boss on her scheme to hoover up the long-term unemployed they gave him two fingers, and Ron Todd, who according to Boris is a good deal better respected by the old guard in Moscow than Comrade Gorbo, said he wasn't going to be told what to do with the Labour Party by a mere politician. Pillock was shunted back to London on the Inter-city with his tail between his legs, the Brothers staying behind to roar the night away singing the Internationale.

The Boss was naturally delighted by Todd falling into her little trap, and orders have now gone out to deprive the TUC of all perks and privileges, e.g. gourmet sandwiches with Fatso next door, not to mention free piss-ups like Noddy and Neddy or whatever they're called.

One of Maurice's skinheads has just banged on the door so I must finish. If you see the old boy, could you tell him that the Boss absolutely agrees with him about flogging off the Post Office, which we all accept is a hot-bed of communists and scrimshankers of every kidney. But when it was mooted and little Ridley worked it out on the back of an envelope Boss got a very angry phone call from Sandringham. The Queen Mum had obviously had a few, and gave Margaret no end of an earful, pointing out that it was the Royal Mail, that her daughter had very few pleasures in life, that the portraits of her on the stamps were very flattering, and she had always been pleased by the thought of being licked by her subjects up and down the country. After that the whole thing was shelved in deference to the Old Lady's age and inebriation and nothing more has been heard of it.

Philately will get you nowhere.

Yours by messenger,

DENIS

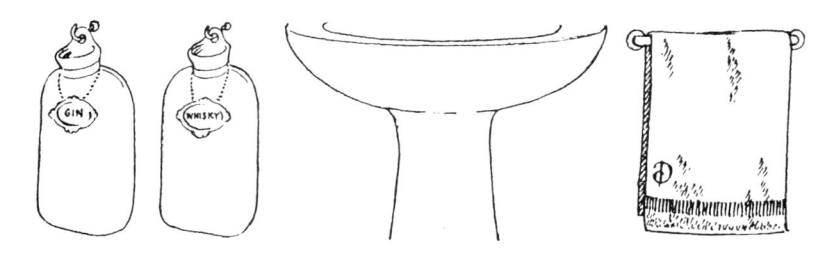

10 Downing Street
Whitehall

30 SEPTEMBER 1988

Dear Bill,

Did Maurice get my obscene greetings from Madrid on his fax machine? I was left alone for hours in the Embassy while the Boss went off to discuss Gibraltar, and the Ambassador very kindly granted me the freedom of his den, complete with half a case of El Matador Knockout Infuriator. By the time I met up with the Boss in the Prado the horizon was performing a rhumba and when somebody mentioned El Greco I remember asking for a large one.

Boss is at present on the warpath, prompted by little Mr Bell, against the U.S. of E. Tinker B. is of the opinion that there are a good many votes to be had out of hammering the Frog, apart from which one whiskery little onion pedlar, Monsieur Zut Alors, has got up her nose in a big way by calling for an end to all customs barriers and full integration under Brussels by 1992. Understandably, M. feels this would do her out of a job, and said as much to her old intellectual chum and master of ceremonies, Jimmy Young, on the wireless a couple of months back.

Blow me, but come the Gathering of the Horny Handed at Bournemouth, Monsieur Alors turned up on the platform, arm in arm with Ron Todd, telling the Brothers in a thick French accent of the Golden Age when the Workers of Europe would unite to do down the Capitalist robber barons with their cigars and top hats. I was with the Boss when Sir Alastair B. announced it on News at Ten, and I have seldom seen her so enraged. 'How dare this snivelling Bolshevik interfere in our affairs?' she carolled, absent-mindedly emptying a largish brownie which I had poured out for myself. 'We did not fight in two world wars to be dictated to by the likes of Monsieur Alors! Denis, refill my glass!' A strange light came into her eyes, and I recognised that another Crusade was about to be launched.

The following morning Greaser Hurd hit the doormat at sparrowfart and was informed in no uncertain terms that he was outraged about the proposed abolition of frontiers. How

'. . . Monsieur Alors turned up on the platform . . .'

did they think, Margaret asked him, that we could arrest IRA terrorists if there were no international barriers? It was on my lips to point out that such international barriers didn't seem to have made a blind bit of difference when it came to rubbing out the Bogtrotter, but I could see Hurd putting on his concerned look and nodding his head like a dog in the back of a car.

Talking of which, you probably saw that the Communists at ITV were finally caught out fabricating evidence against our gallant boys in the SAS. The Boss had said all along that the programme should never have been allowed, and now it turns out that they bribed a waiter to make it all up. Luckily the rug is going to be pulled from under those fat cats at ITV any minute now, and Lord Young has been instructed to draw up plans for dismantling all their Agitprop 'current affairs' programmes once and for all, so that we can watch Italian lady strip-tease artists beamed in round the clock from Rome. I've ordered my dish already from Maurice's new firm PicSat. They were originally part of a cancelled arms shipment to Abu Dhabi, but apparently you just clip them on the chimney, turn on, and it's all a very far cry from Sandy Gall.

Howe's been behaving pretty oddly recently. I don't know whether you saw him in the paper giving the clenched fist salute to a lot of Commie Freedom Fighters in Mozambique. He was sloping about in his brothel creepers after he got back gazing wistfully at the typing pool, and I button-holed him on the way into the den. 'If we're best friends with PWB, how come we're rooting for the Red Fuzzies out in the bush?' Howe gave a little cough, obviously stumped, said he really hadn't got time to go into it in any detail, and shuffled on into his morning session of Listen to Mother.

However, I was talking to some Foreign Office bird in the Club, and he said they were all as baffled as I was. No one had asked Howe to go on this tour, and it wasn't even winter time, which is when they usually like to take off on a freebie to warmer climes. If you ask me, Howe is definitely in love, and with that type of pretty buttoned-up lawyer cove, it can manifest itself in all kinds of strange ways. You remember our QC friend in Deal who strangled himself in the Oxfam shop for love of that very fat manageress at Tesco's.

According to Boris, Margaret and Tinker B. were very pleased with their SDP sleeper 'Dr O'. The plan to splinter all the silly parties in the middle is bang on course, and as far as Boris can tell, no one has rumbled that the Doctor is our man.

The conference is looming up. I wouldn't go near Brighton if I were you. The whole town will be sealed off and there's talk of nerve gas being used by the SAS if any of the alarm bells ring.

Yours in the bulletproof underpants,

DENIS

THE GRAND BRIGHTON

14 OCTOBER 1988

Dear Bill,

As you see, we've finally made it back here to the reconstructed bomb-site. I took a stroll along the Prom just now in the company of three plainclothes SAS (one disguised as a woman pushing a pram), ten uniformed policemen and three plain vanloads of assorted gorillas with machine-guns kerb-crawling a few paces behind. It was just like the wartime. (Do you remember when we were stationed at Bexhill?) Barbed wire in coils all along the beach, lumps of concrete sunk into the shingle, those skull and crossbones notices to indicate mines, and radar trucks every fifty yards with bowls going round and round on the roof. I asked Soldier P. whether they weren't perhaps overdoing it and I got very short shrift when I suggested a quick one in the Old Boot. There was a lot of yak yak and crackle on the walkie-talkies, white tapes were laid all the way to the pub door, the drinkers in the Saloon spreadeagled against the outside wall with their arms up for a body search, and sniffer-dogs bussed in to check the cellar. When I got round to buying my large brownie Mine Host was spitting tintacks. Any hope of getting out to Pyecombe to smite the prune was clearly a non-starter.

It all began on the Sunday night when Margaret and I were driven in a black-windowed limo to Op. HQ at Hillingdon, where Brass hats were waiting for us with sandtables and diagrammatic maps of Brighton. Young Turk in charge saluted, and then as we took our seats, dimmed the lights and spelt out the scenario. I could see the Boss was tickled pink by all this, as she always gets very hyped up by anything that reminds her of Falklands days. 'Prime Minister, to give you a brief Sitrep. Ulster Int. Q. 1 reports seventeen IRA units planning an amphibious invasion using Libyan submarines to hit the Marina at 0300 hours Thursday. They will regroup at the Conference Centre disguised as loyal Tory ladies as you

'. . . I took a stroll along the Prom . . .'

are beginning your keynote speech.' 'They must not win, they must not win!' Margaret breathed passionately, her eyes glowing in the reflected light from the briefing board. 'Quite so, Prime Minister. Sunray, i.e. Brigadier Longbond here, will therefore oversee Operation Bogstop, which will go at 00.01 hours on Monday morning.'

The Brigadier then began to cover the board with felt symbols representing tanks, helicopter units, infantry battalions etc, and explained the way in which they would assist the civil power. At the end of it I was dying for a drink, but the Boss seemed well pleased, and I could see Longbond and his Merry Men being marked down for gongs and knighthoods come the New Year.

As I write, M. is still in the bathroom with her chief gag-writer Sir Custardface (a.k.a. Sir Ronald Millar) and Tinkerbell, thrashing out the final draft of her Big Speech. Sir

Custardface bearded me in the Alhaji Bar earlier on to try out a few jokes about Kinnock, e.g. 'Ladies and Gentlemen, pray silence for the Leader of Her Majesty's Opposition and Mrs Ron Todd' – I didn't understand that one at all – 'We shall fudge, fudge and fudge again' (Hooter) and finally 'Kinnock, Kinnock, who's there? Answer: Mr Gorbachov.' (Prolonged raspberry from Yours Truly and suggestion that he kindly leave the Bar.) If you ask me, they may have to get a new gag-writer in, as the old boy is obviously a bit past it.

Meanwhile Tinkerbell is very excited about the new Green campaign, designed to give Margaret even longer shelf life. For my money it's a non-starter, and Ridley absolutely agrees with me. We had it all at Burmah, with a lot of bearded trouble-makers saying our marine paints division was single-handedly wiping out life on the seabed, and we were rendering the air unbreathable with our two-stroke. All patently ridiculous, I mean I've been smoking seventy a day since I was five, hanging over toxic chemicals all my working life, and I can still go round Huntercombe in 82. However the Boss has been converted to the marketing potential of the Organic Armpits Brigade, especially now that the Royalty are so hot on all that kind of caper, and Cecil has told her it's the best bet for launching more nuclear power-stations ('nice clean things with no nasty smoke') and flogging off the Water to Maurice Picarda and Co. ('Making Private Water Cleaner'). By the by, Cecil is still on course to take over from Fatty come the next Night of the Long Knives and is doing an evening course in TV Elocution and Book-Keeping.

Don't blame me if this is a bit late arriving. They've blocked up all the letterboxes, and some wretched PC Plod from the local force is even now in the foyer waiting to bicycle over a half full sack to the railway station. All trains stop at Hassocks after which commuters are invited to continue their journey on foot through the various check-points.

See you when we get back to town. I've reserved a table at the RAC on the 19th for Maurice's Coming Out Party. He hasn't enjoyed the Clinic at all this time and I think the old fellow deserves a bit of a beano.

Yours on Sus,

DENIS

10 Downing Street
Whitehall

28 OCTOBER 1988

Dear Bill,

I had Maurice in tears after lunch at the RAC on Thursday. He'd apparently shipped over a hundred thousand pirated copies of *Spycatcher* from Holland in paperback and can't now shift them for love or money. He has some crazy scheme for giving them away as an inducement to join his new Love Classics Book Club, but I can't see the punters rising to it.

I don't know if you saw old Ozzie Wright on the box, but he was making about as much sense as Maurice was after lunch and could hardly remember his own name. The long and the short of it was that it might all have been a dream, with him plotting to bring down Harold Wilson. Judging from his circumstances as shown on TV, i.e. tumbledown woodshed in the outback with Mother boiling his socks on the range – his cheque has still to come through. And the Boss is all the more determined to deprive him of his ill-gotten gains. She was livid when the Judges finally decided there was no harm in the old boy, and there was the usual summons to the striped trousered brigade to turn up pretty smartish at HQ to receive their regular dose of gamma rays. I saw Mayhew, who took over from Havers when he'd had one lunch too many, and he said they were pretty confident they could nail Wright for breach of copyright. The money they're all making from the affair will keep them in claret for years, so they don't give a toss either way as long as it goes on.

You probably saw what happened to poor old Munster when he tried to make a few honest bob out of his memoirs *I Was a Teenage Werewolf*. No sooner had his publishers got the copies stacked in the window at Hatchards, than up pops little Miss Keays surrounded by grave men of the law, demanding redress. Huge cheques change hands, crack of champagne corks ringing through the Inns of Court until the small hours, and poor Munster has to sit up all night with a pair of nail scissors cutting out page 109. I happened to overhear Margaret on the phone to smarmy Cecil for their usual nightly chinwag, and she was smoothing his ruffled feathers. 'Of course you will

'. . . Munster has to sit up all night with a pair of nail scissors cutting out page 109 . . .'

have Nigel's job, my dear, and I know Norman was only trying to cause mischief, but we can't have little Miss Whatsername cropping up again and again, can we Cecil?' I could hear Smarmy C. on the other end sobbing his reassurances that he was sure he'd seen the back of her this time. It crossed my mind that he might eventually take a leaf out of that poor old pooftah's book and hire a hit-man to rub her out.

As you may have seen on News for the Deaf Hurd was sent out on to the doorstep again, this time to announce a ban on all party politicals by the IRA. As he was coming back in I asked him why, if it was such a good idea, it had taken them twenty years to think of it, and he went very red in the face.

He said *entre nous* that M. had demanded a twelve-point plan to beat the IRA, that ten of them had been thrown out as entirely absurd, including putting tranquillisers in the Ulster water supply, and now that public execution by the SAS was proving a bit iffy, the ban was the only one that would get off the ground. Of course it's backfired. World-wide publicity for the IRA, all the reptiles up in arms, the do-gooders like old Scarman talking about freedom of speech in a democracy, and Fatso Hattersley made to appear statesmanlike and intelligent.

By the by, didn't you think Sir Custardface came up trumps this year with his two jokes for the Big Speech at Brighton? Joke Number One: 'I say, I say, I say, what is Kinnock's favourite Frank Sinatra song?' Answer: 'I did it HER way.' (Two minutes' standing ovation.) Joke Number Two: 'What would be a better name for the SDP?' Answer: 'SOS.' (Audience crashes about weeping and breaking furniture, St John's Ambulance Brigade move in to carry out coronary cases.)

Talking of jokes, was that you very drunk on the blower late on Saturday night offering me the editorship of *Punch*? I might have fallen for it, but nobody can seriously be offering money like that outside Kuwait.

Yours with the hump,

DENIS

DINERSCLUBHOTEL WARSAW

11 NOVEMBER 1988

Dear Bill,

I can tell you this is a pretty dismal place. Very like Wolverhampton during the war: factory chimneys smoking away, RC skypilots beetling about in those funny black hats with a bobble on top, people queuing to buy a packet of fags, snorts in short supply and no golf courses whatsoever.

I rather take my hat off to this new PM chap they've brought in, Mr Radetsky. The Boss had lined up a crusading whistle-stop, the highlight of which was to be her standing arm in arm with muttonchops Walewski in the shipyard. No fool Brother Radetsky: he saw himself being upstaged by a woman in a fur hat, and immediately closed down the shipyard. This, as you can imagine, caused a bit of a flutter in the Henhouse and little Tinkerbell was summoned late at night from his table at the Acid House. Howe had already shimmered in upon receipt of the news with an entourage of wooftahs from the FO, and explained the situation to the bemused Bell. At first the Boss refused to admit that there was any problem. 'Surely, Geoffrey, this is what we have always warned about, poor Mr Walencia is being crushed under the heel of the Communist Jackboot. Even more important that I should visit him, if necessary in his little home, to show the West cares.'

'But Prime Minister,' interposed the First Fairy, 'could it not be said, unfairly and uncharitably of course, that the Polish Prime Minister has taken a leaf from your book, and that his arguments for closure are identical to those you yourself produced for introducing redundancies in Sunderland.' At this the Boss's eyes flashed. 'What nonsense!' she cried, 'we are talking here about an authoritarian regime blowing out the faintly flickering flame of freedom.'

Hence the firm set to her jaw as she toddled down the steps of the RAF Hercules to shout 'Hello Soldiers' to the Guard of Honour, who in turn shouted something back, no doubt offensive. We were then driven off to the Palace of International Harmony for a thimbleful of warm vodka and a disgusting banquet of pickled sausage and red cabbage washed down with something terrible called Bull's Pisz. I was stuck next to a woman with red elbows and a face like a potato who used to throw the hammer in the Olympics. After several hours of small talk, Radetsky rose to his feet and proposed a toast to our esteemed visitor who has shown the way out of the economic labyrinth, a heroine of the post-industrial struggle – so the interpreter repeated po-faced with a slight Scottish burr – who had not flinched from closing down uneconomic shipyards. More important, she had shown the single-mindedness and courage to confront the union bully-boys who were seeking to undermine the democratically elected government with the power of mob rule.

This was greeted with a roar of applause. Five hundred Poles together with their stout wives stood as one to shout 'Miss Zetchsh!', down half a gallon of Bull's Pisz and throw their glasses into the fireplace. While the scraping of chairs and shouting continued, I saw Margaret taking a quick squint under the table at her notes and then tearing them decisively in half. When she finally got up in response to deafening drumming on the table from the swarthy Polaks her face was a study of conflicting emotions. After thanking them for their warm reception, she contented herself with a few rather generalised reflections on the benefits of privatisation and pushing back the frontiers of state control, and sat down looking like thunder.

None of this boded too well for the two hundred miles up a potholed single-track 'motorway' to Danzig for our meeting with Mr Muttonchops, the Polish Arthur Scargill. The old boy seems to do quite well out of the Western media and he found me a bottle of Glen Morangie behind the wardrobe. He has a huge picture of the Boss over his bed alongside the Pope (Would you believe? I think, *entre nous*, it may have been pinned up for the occasion), and knelt down to kiss M's hand as she arrived at the front door. 'We look to you, Mother Thatcher, as the saviour of our shipyards,' he said in Polish, his voice choking with emotion, 'as the champion of workers' rights. We believe that the shipwrights of Gdansk can form a cooperative . . .'

I could see the Boss fidgeting a bit as the woman interpreter relayed all this into her good ear within range of the TV microphones. 'Just one minute, Mr Welensky,' she insisted, 'I think you must remember that there is no place in the world of today for Socialism of any kind. I hope you understand that. Does he?' The interpreter repeated her message to the kneeling hero of the Counter-Revolution, and large tears began to trickle down his rosy old cheeks. M. paused for two or three photographs, waving away a bevy of priests attempting to bless her, and we made our rapid escape.

Meanwhile back at the ranch poor old Matey next door has hastened the day of his replacement by smarmy Cecil. In the Boss's absence he shot his mouth off to a few reptiles about his plans to give the OAPs a short sharp shock by taking away their perks, and not surprisingly all the wets rose up demanding his head on a charger. The Boss (who incidentally agrees with him a hundred percent) pretended to be shocked and muttered something to me about Nigel suffering from strain and needing a complete change of scene.

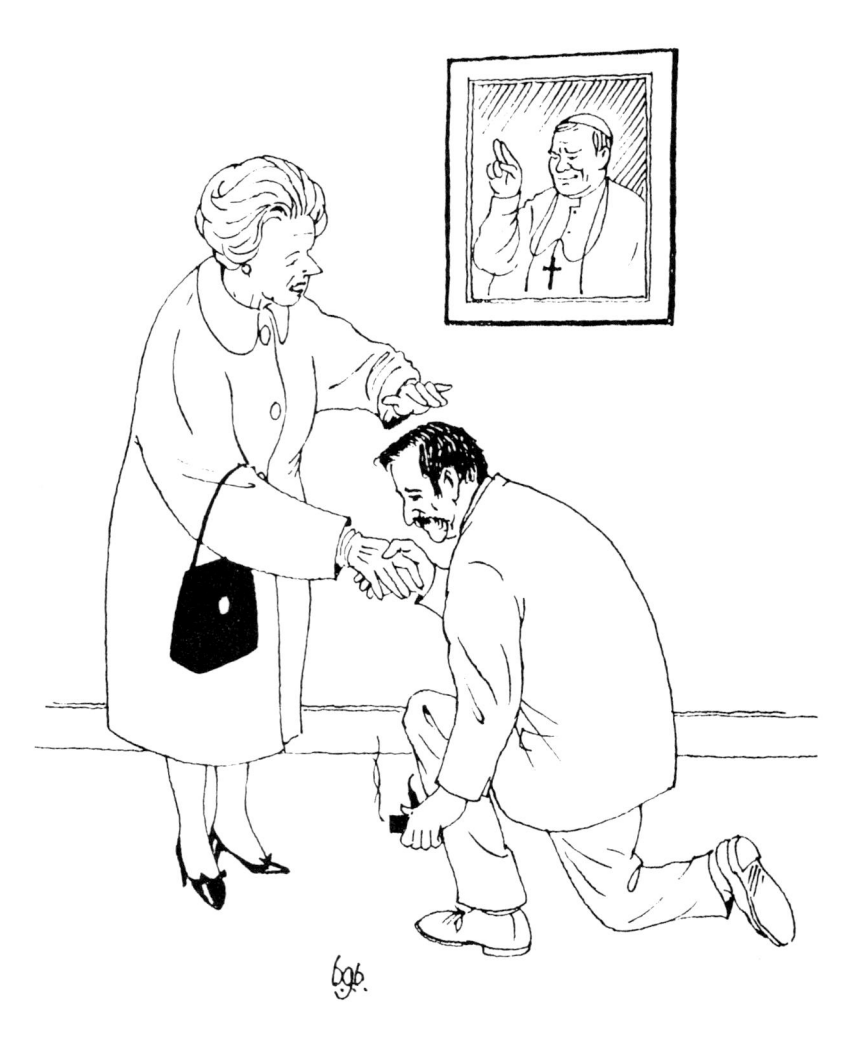

'. . . and knelt down to kiss M's hand . . .'

I'm sorry to hear about Maurice's firework party. That was rather a nice old church. I am told that immersion in a bucket of petroleum jelly is very good for burns about the hinder parts. Perhaps you could pass this on to the Cottage Hospital.
Yours in Solidarity,

DENIS

10 Downing Street
Whitehall

25 NOVEMBER 1988

Dear Bill,

Jetlag can have an extraordinary effect on a man. I could have sworn I saw Fatty next door digging a hole in his back garden by the light of a hurricane lamp, burying what looked like several cassettes of recording tape. However in the morning the grass appeared to be untouched and I can only assume that I was hallucinating after hours of insomnia.

By the way, when we meet for our Xmas shindig at Frant remind me to put Hoppo's parting gift in the back of the car – a signed photograph of the Old Gunslinger and the emaciated spouse in a Texas silver frame, six foot by four. I thought it could make one of those prizes in Daphne's Draw for the Seals.

The PR boys in Washington had obviously been planning last week's business for months as the final scene in the Hopalong Cassidy Story (From Hollywood to Eternity) in which the old boy, now slightly stooping and with the first flecks of grey sprayed on to his temples, totters out on to the White House steps to receive the acclaim of thousands of cheering world leaders.

What we hadn't bargained for was that the Boss had been billed as the Leading Lady, the Emaciated S. having been deemed insufficiently photogenic in recent screen tests. No expenses had been spared, the child Carol being called upon to skip her weekly visit to the Job Centre and be jetted in, and the Boy Mark, despite all my pleading, released from the Burgerdorf custody to be with us for a 'happy family reunion'. Enough to throw a pall over things, I think you will agree, but we hadn't seen nothing yet. As our RAF Lancaster touched down at John Foster Dulles Airbase, a terrifying array of giant male majorettes in enormous shoulder-pads and dangling gold chains began swaggering up and down and twirling batons to the tune of 'Hello Dolly'. While the Boss and I inspected this shower of crop-headed wooftahs, all twice our height and making us look bloody ridiculous, Hoppo was signalled to be approaching in his electrified beach-buggy. As soon as the

'. . . embraced the Boss effusively . . .'

prompter screen had been erected, he mounted the podium, embraced the Boss effusively, greeted me warmly as 'Prince Philip', and turned awkwardly to read from the screen.

I may say I have had to listen to some pretty good bilge, in private and in public, from those who have fallen under Margaret's spell, but this took the biscuit. Not since Sir Churchill, he began, had so great a statesman bestridden the Western World. 'We look to you, Margaret' – at this point the crystals began to work and tears brimmed – 'as a shining beacon. Your courage, your steadfastness, your leadership as Prime Minister of, er, England has inspired and will inspire countless millions yet unborn to lisp your name in tandem with Mother Teresa of, er, India . . .' The Boss, who had begun by drumming her fingers impatiently on her handbag, now warmed to this treacly serenade from the Student President, and when it came to her turn shed all her inhibitions to give as good as she got, calling him 'Mr Wonderful' and crediting him with ushering in a golden age that would last at least five hundred years.

Barely time to have a pee at the Embassy, snorts of a most perfunctory nature, and into the bib and tucker for the most ballsaching dinner of all time. Yours Truly put his foot in it right away when introduced to his companion at table, a ghastly white-haired old bat of wrinkly countenance called Mrs Bush, whom I congratulated on her son's triumph. 'No, Mr Thatcher, I am not the President Elect's mother, I am his wife. But how charming of you to think him so youthful.' I gave up at this point and turned my attention to a member of the British artistic riff-raff who had been corralled in for the night, one Mrs Lloyd-Webber, who claimed to be richer than the Queen but otherwise didn't seem to be one of nature's intellectuals and spent most of the dinner raising and lowering her eyelashes. Bang opposite, just my luck, was the most awful Bertie from somewhere up north with platinum blond hair and funny glasses who had apparently made a fortune out of naughty calendars for the gay community. Just as we were about to lower our snouts into the trough after grace had been said by Billy Graham, Bush himself came up to clap us all on the back, shake our hands, and enquire 'Hi! Been getting some ass lately?' I was told afterwards this was part of his election-winning routine, designed to find favour with the great unwashed. The only one who said 'Yes' was Mr Hockney opposite, which didn't surprise me in the least. This beano was followed by more tearful speeches, featuring Basil Bush and his little friend Danny the Quail, who was only allowed to rise on his feet for a second or two at the end and say 'Right on!' for fear of provoking another Wall Street Crash.

Meanwhile back home, we have our very own Fattygate Scandal warming up nicely, with Nigel accused of evidence-shredding over the benefits to the Poor and Needy at this

Christmastide. According to Boris who had some kind of listening device in the room, Lawson told the journalists he was going to target the Oldies and then go down some road or other making a few cuts – with many a nudge and wink, as is customary at these briefings. The drunken reptiles then spilled out into the street and scrambled into the nearest telephone box hollering about the Scoop of the Century. Fatty, who had apparently OD'd on the Muesli, came round, immediately panicked, announced a big handout, and then recorded Highlights from the Wonderful World of the Opera all over the offending tape.

Luckily Pillock was so busy with his Green preoccupations that he failed to make much of it, but Fatty's stock is now plummeting, and Smarmy C's frightful wife has been round measuring the curtains at Number 11.

Maurice is coming up to town on Thursday to sell his satellite dishes in Oxford Street. Any chance of our getting together over a tray or two of RAC port?

That's all, Folks,

DENIS

10 Downing Street Whitehall

9 DECEMBER 1988

Dear Bill,

No, that wasn't me you saw lying in the bushes at the foot of Mont Saint-Michel. Apparently one of the reptiles overimbibed, lost his balance while taking a photograph and had to be given the kiss of life by a member of the Gendarmerie. The whole thing came as a complete surprise to me. M. informed me that morning over breakfast she was choppering off for some Euroconfab that would bore the arse off me and that there would be something cold in the deep freeze. Next thing I knew, dozing over the TV with a large brownie in hand, up she pops on the Mont having an Awayday with her fancy-man Monsieur Mitterand.

'... one of the reptiles ... had to be given the kiss of life by a member of the Gendarmerie ...'

I couldn't help but smile when the old boy, having smothered her hands in French kisses, had a bit of a turn as they laboured up the Pilgrims' Way towards the four-star Crêperie de Madame Blezard, and had to sit down. Boss looked very scornful at this sign of weakness and plodded on to the crest. She was already well stuck in to the Frog's Leg Soup and Mashed Garlic by the time Maurice Chevalier arrived looking pale and sweaty.

If you ask me there's nobody else in the whole Eurolot who cares for her at all, otherwise she wouldn't waste her time with him. You probably saw she threw a fit when the Belgies refused to hand over that bomb-slinging God-botherer Father O'Ryan, claiming she hadn't filed the right particulars. M. and Mayhew were a bit caught off balance by this, Ingham was hauled in, and it transpired they had filled the form in wrong. While the three of them were trying to think of something to say, little Haughey of course seized the initiative and started twitting her with not knowing what she was talking about. He then really got her hopping mad by failing to turn up at a meeting in Rhodes where he was billed for a wigging.

Meanwhile El Fatso, according to Boris, has lived to fight another day, as Smarmy C. still hasn't finished his evening classes in O-level economics. Poor Old Matey lumbered round early last week looking a bit crestfallen, refrained from any personal abuse when I let him in the front door, and even asked me to be a good chap and go and get him a very large drink. By the time I got back he was spilling the beans to Margaret about the record deficit and saying it was only a freak. 'Freak's the word, Mr Lawson, and you are that freak!' she exploded. 'I told you before, you made a grave mistake cutting taxes in your last budget. I have been on the line to the United States, talking to Professor Walters, whose bed I may say is waiting for him upstairs, and he says the only solution now is to put up interest rates.' 'I have done that, Prime Minister. If you will listen to me for a moment . . .' 'I am glad to hear that you heed his advice. You know how much I value Professor Walters's opinions, and it is a welcome change to see you obeying him so unquestioningly. No, do not interrupt, come with me.' With this she took the unwilling Bunter by the arm and propelled him through the front door into a waiting armoured car en route for Halitosis Hall.

I only heard highlights from the debate while I was shaving the following morning, but the Smellysocks have finally come up with a bright little Featherweight called Smith or possibly Brown who danced into the ring and poked Fatso a couple of quite nasty ones in the ribs. As if this wasn't enough, the Great White Whale E. Heath rose from the depths to rub her nose in it, saying that she shouldn't be surprised if the Belgians failed to hop the first time she cracked her whip.

Furniss was very cock-a-hoop about the Interest Rates when

I bowled in to run an eye over the figures at the NatWest. He found quite a decent couple of bottles of North African Infuriator, and advised me after a glass or two not to touch Lord Young's prospectus with a barge pole. British Steel in his opinion had done a bit of creative accountancy to make it look OK to the unwary overseas punter, but once it got on the road the sawdust would start coming out of the tyres p.d.q. I asked him about Smarmy C's Power Launch, but he said if you read the small print it was all a balls-up, electricity would cost ten times as much as it does in any other country on earth, industry would be forced to put their prices up, and by the time Smarmy C. moved into Number 11 the whole shebang would be down the Swanee.

His conclusion, as we polished off the second bottle, was that anyone in his right mind with a bit of loose change would look at 13 per cent and bang it away on a year's deposit, certainly not squander it on madcap schemes to destroy Socialism for ever.

Talking of madcap schemes, I got a call from Marlborough Street Police Station late on Friday night to say that a Mr Peshawar had been taken into charge for obstructing the highway in Oxford Street with a dump truck full of Japanese satellite dishes causing a tailback as far as Notting Hill in one direction and Islington in the other. He had furthermore attempted to sell same to the Constable arresting him for trading without a truck's licence. Maurice, when I found him, was still in festive mood, entertaining the cells with his version of 'My Way'. However they've now told him that he will, thanks to some new legislation brought in by the jack-booted nanny Hurd, have to pass a medical before he can ever drive again.

I've persuaded the Boss's driver, Symons, to drive me round to Lillywhite's for the Christmas shopping on Tuesday morning. If you'd care to show outside the Bunker at tennish I'd be very happy to have you along in the back seat. Apparently they've got these new Jap robot drink dispensers that carry up to four gallons and follow you round the golf course pouring out a large one every time you snap your fingers.

Are you on?
Yours in Pre-Christmas Tension,

DENIS

10 Downing Street
Whitehall

23 DECEMBER 1988

Dear Bill,

I'm glad you enjoyed our outing to Lillywhite's. Where did we have lunch? If you have any recollection at all I'd be very grateful if you'd give me a bell as I left various articles of clothing in the Gents along with that parcel of golf paraphernalia which was going to be my present to the Major.

You'll be pleased to hear I had a word with Lawson later in the day. I ran into him at pre-Christmas snorts for the Coolies at Central Office and told him that Lillywhite's was like the Black Hole of Calcutta, Japs and assorted riff-raff climbing over one another like baboons waving their credit cards, all the shelves stripped bare — what price his so-called curb on spending the noo? As usual very condescending, expression of amused contempt: 'You wouldn't understand, Denis, it takes some time for measures of this kind to filter through the retail interface, but to give you one specific example' — here he selected a twelve-inch cigar and lit up — 'Moss Bross, a very old firm, are having a pre-Christmas sale. I think you can tell your drunken friends at the Club that this could well be a straw in the wind.' I contemplated asking him whether they were doing anything of the kind at High and Mighty, that store that caters for Extra Outsize and the Obese, but thought better of it.

I am glad to say that the Currie woman has finally been given the push. You probably saw on News for the Deaf that she shot her mouth off once too often — farmers up in arms, millions of chickens strangled, eggs shipped off to starving Armenians — and being a woman like some others who spring to mind (no n. no p.d.) little Mrs Poppadum refused to admit for a moment that she might have been wrong. The Boss was all against throwing her off the sledge, but when the writs began to fly the wolves finally got their breakfast. The odd thing, according to the Major whose friend Marjoribanks runs a broiler farm outside Maidstone, is that the Currie bird for once had got the right end of the stick and egg-guzzlers are dropping off the perch at a rate of knots. However, as he says, when the farming lobby calls for blood, they get it.

Our friend the Teasock has continued to run true to form. The sight of Margaret going purple in the face whenever he appears has given his image in the Emerald Isle a terrific boost, and he is now the most popular Irishman since Phil the Fluter. What really got M's goat was the suggestion that the Reverend O'Bombflinger wouldn't get a fair trial over here after she'd branded him the world's most wanted war criminal. She immediately blew her top in Halitosis Hall, saying that it was an insult to every man woman and child in Britain. The Bogtrotters then offered to lay on a trial for Father O'B in Dublin, whereupon friend Mayhew was wound up and set off across the table repeating the phrase 'No British witness would be safe walking the streets of Dublin at night', which leaves them all back at Square One, precisely where they started out.

It's a bit hard to make out the Boss's thinking on terrorism, quite frankly. I mean, at the same time she's ranting away about the Men of Violence in Dublin, this frightful little Middle-Eastern Bertie, Ararat, appears to have her full support. As you may remember he was billed to play the UN in New York for a one-night stand some weeks back, and got the bum's rush from Hopalong. At worldwide popular request the venue was changed to the Geneva Palais de Danse. M. appeared to play it very crafty, lining up at the time with Hoppo as his sole supporter on earth, and then changing her mind p.d.q. when Hoppo said he was all right after all. She is now claiming that she supported Ararat all along, and that she was single-handedly responsible for making Hoppo see sense. If you'd seen Hopalong recently you'd realise this was a contradiction in terms. He clearly has no idea where he is for ninety per cent of the time and wouldn't know Ararat from a bar of soap.

You mention Christmas. I wish you hadn't. Wu rang from Chequers last night to say the central heating was on the blink again, there was water coming in through the roof of the Blue Room, and that daft boy who does the pruning had sheared through the main telephone line. Quite frankly I don't believe a word of it. I think he's hoping we'll call it off and he won't have to stir his idle Chinese stumps. Anyway the usual black sheep have been invited, including our daughter Carol, who you probably saw got into trouble trying to smuggle in my

'. . . the venue was changed to
the Geneva Palais de Danse . . .'

Christmas present, a big fancy watch from America that lights up, plays 'I'm Dreaming of a White Christmas', and prints out recipes for making Hotshots. I wasn't too concerned when I learned it had been confiscated.

I think I may be able to see a window on Boxing Day when Mother Howe comes round with her mince pies and I can plead Salmonella.

Yours under the mistletoe,

DENIS

10 Downing Street
Whitehall

6 JANUARY 1989

Dear Bill,

Sorry your car broke down on the M40 on the way back from our Chequers Xmas lunch. The behaviour of the RAC man sounds to have been bloody typical, and I'm not surprised you gave him a black eye. After you'd left, very wisely in my view, things rather degenerated. Sir Custardface got very maudlin, took me into the library and put his arm round my shoulders, telling me he knew only too well his jokes at the Conference hadn't been any good, but he was finding it harder and harder as the years went by and if the Boss felt the time had come to call in Bill Oddie then he would entirely understand. As I predicted, the little black sheep Archer turned up later on, cocky as ever, and stayed until half past eleven, regaling us with anecdotes about his three-minute mile at Oxford. Mr Wu, who as you saw had been hitting Mitterand's Christmas Hamper fairly regularly between bouts at the hot stove, suddenly reeled into the room after dinner, kow-towed to friend Archer and asked him if he'd like to meet his sister. 'You likee, velly nice girl, velly clean. Hee hee hee.' Luckily the Boss was deep in conversation with our unspeakable daughter-in-law, the pregnant Miss Burgerdorf, and I was able to bustle Wu back to his kitchen and throw a bucket of cold water over him.

Gone midnight I was just finishing the heel-taps and trying to lock up when I came upon the Boss closeted in the Falkender Suite with our snuff-taking friend, Master Bell. They both appeared to have had a good deal to drink and surprisingly keen for me to join their conflab. Bell produced a half-finished bottle of my own Four Star Marquis de Sade 'Paralyser' Cognac which I brought back from the Duty Free after our day at Longchamps in 1968. 'Now Denis,' he beamed expansively, tapping the ash off his cigar into Wu's Chinese Christmas Crib, 'we're throwing a few things up the flagpole to see if anybody's there. New campaign is the name of the game. How does "Go Divine in 89" grab you?' My jaw may have dropped a fraction, and he continued to outline an extraordinary scenario featuring Margaret as some kind of TV Evangelist, bringing back the old values and putting God back on the payroll. I must say it struck me as a damnfool idea, the Boss banging her tambourine and threatening the punters with hell-fire if they didn't quit their wicked ways and vote Conservative p.d.q.

I think I must have passed out in the middle of all this. Two or three days later I found myself in the back seat of the limo hours before dawn en route to a tryst at some Godforsaken dump with egg-cups on the roof where that randy Ambassador chap Jay used to hang out with all those floozies. Sliding doors revealed that frightful groveller Frost rubbing his palms and bowing. 'Super, super, super, Prime Minister! What a truly gigantic honour to receive on this, the first day of a new year, in our humble studios! And the consort no less, Mr Thatcher, sir! What a great honour and privilege!' It was all I could do not to throw up as he ushered us into the sofa-strewn studio and began reading the tele-prompting device with a terrible intensity. 'This year, Prime Minister, you celebrate your tenth year of office, a truly unique achievement in our annals.' The camera then showed the Boss smiling and showing off her new Mister Softie perm by Henri of Great Missenden. 'May I join with a grateful nation in paying tribute to your astonishing powers of vision and leadership.' All this was clearly too much for the Boss, and by the time Frostie got to the questions little Bell had put on the teleprompter for him about whether she'd

'... Bell produced a half-finished bottle of my own Four Star Marquis de Sade "Paralyser" Cognac ...'

ever had a religious experience, the Old Girl fluffed her lines, and left out a long bit about her sense of being called to lead the nation back into the paths of righteousness.

Did you see Lawson's New Year message to the Troops? Everything tickety-boo, right on course, inflation about to make a soft landing. My instinct, confirmed by Furniss, after watching it, was to shift everything abroad, or failing that into the Building Society as they're the only people who are going to do well. I suppose 14 per cent is tough on first time buyers, but my advice has always been to pay cash down, and it's their own damn fault if they get themselves into trouble borrowing.

Talking of messages, HM the Q has sent a sharp note to the Boss telling her that next time there's a big air crash can she please have time to re-record her Christmas Message, and what's more would Margaret kindly cut out her Florence Nightingale malarkey, and leave that sort of thing to the pros? Boss is fuming over this, and is planning further curtailment of the Royal Freebies in the coming year.

See you at Maurice's Epiphany Car Boot Sale. 'Turn Your Unwanted Christmas Presents Into Hard Cash.'

Yours in receipt of Custom,

DENIS

10 Downing Street Whitehall

20 JANUARY 1989

Dear Bill,

Sorry to miss you in Rye. The Major and I turned up at the last minute and Mr Pilbeam the manager at the Mermaid gave me a rather shirty look, no doubt recalling the last time I took Maurice there, when he left two baths running all night, punched an American woman in the lift and sent the grapefruit back with a cigar stubbed out in it. Long and the short of it was they told us they were fully booked.

You ask about relationships with the Palace, and I must tell you, *entre nous*, that things have come to a pretty pass. H.M.'s nose was already out of joint about the Boss vetoing her trip to Russia, then one of her Palace Poofters climbed on the blower to say that protocol had been breached by Margaret's habit of rushing to the scene of any disaster when tradition dictated that the Monarch or her chosen representative should get first crack of the whip. The Boss, as I think I told you, was fit to be tied, and went on for most of the night about who the public wanted at moments of national grief – 'a caring focus of unity. They don't want a remote royal personage with

'. . . The Major and I turned up at the last minute and Mr Pilbeam gave me rather a shirty look . . .'

no idea of day to day reality, they want one of their own kind, a simple mother on her way from the supermarket. Wouldn't you, Denis, if you were struck down in the prime of life?' I was about to answer, but Margaret pressed on with the rhetorical questions and I think I must have eventually dozed off.

Of course what the Palace doesn't realise is that the Boss has established a top-secret Disaster Hot Line in Whitehall, so that if so much as a gas-stove explodes anywhere in the British Isles she can be in a car and on the way there with a full TV crew well in advance of any Royalty. So when there was yet another plane crash on the M1 the Old Girl was in full spate on all three channels before the Woofs of the Bedchamber had even opened their *Daily Telegraphs*. Result the Royals didn't get a look in at all. Boss triumphant. 'Well, what do they expect?' she crowed as she returned from the Intensive Care with a huge fluffy toy from the Fire Brigade for Mark's baby, 'Gallivanting about the globe sunbathing and taking skiing holidays when there is work to be done. It is something I intend to raise with Her Majesty at our next weekly meeting.'

As you know, the Boss is constitutionally obliged to have a regular chinwag with the monarch, top secret of course, when she spells out what they're up to in words of one syllable. On this occasion I couldn't help observing on her return that she was looking very flushed and grumpy, and had obviously had a big helping of cold tongue pie. 'Get Hurd!' she shouted as she slammed the front door and within minutes the bespectacled ex-paperback novelist was nodding earnestly like a dog in the back of a car. 'Competition, Douglas. It's the main plank of our policy. What did we tell the BBC? Set your house in order, or other people will do it better. Now everyone is buying their dish, and a good thing too.' I was about to point out that Maurice's efforts at pushing the aforesaid equipment in Oxford Street had met with a pretty big thumbs-down from the punters, when she went on. 'The Royal Family must learn the same lesson. They are dependent on public funds for their very comfortable way of life. Professionals can do it better, and I will not be dictated to by a woman whose political experience is limited to opening international garden fetes.'

'Ahem, aha,' coughed the Home Office apparatchik, 'I would counsel caution, Prime Minister. The latest polls, and more importantly, figures on invisible imports from tourism, would suggest the Royal Family are still very popular . . .' 'All very well, Douglas, so long as they don't interfere in politics. They have no right at all to usurp my prerogative, and make capital out of other people's sufferings. And send Parkinson in, he still hasn't grasped the point about the Ozone Layer.' One pinstriped chancer gave way to another, and I gathered from the *Telegraph* the next morning that Smarmy C. had been told to do a rapid about-turn, and is now right behind the campaign for Sizewell B, C and D.

As part of little Bell's 'Go Divine in 89' campaign we were finally browbeaten into accepting a three-year-old invitation from Lambeth Palace. I took the precaution of having three or four large brownies before we sallied forth, and sure enough when we arrived there was only a thimbleful of warm Cyprus sherry to strengthen one for the ordeal ahead, i.e. Mother Runcie's Greek Pot-au-Feu in the Thomas Cranmer Ballroom. We all stood awkwardly round the Oxford College placemats while Runcie fumbled with his pectoral cross, bowed his head, and muttered something to the effect that before we got stuck into the very tired-looking supermarket pâté before us 'we should not forget the starving, the homeless, those unemployed, etcetera etcetera,' by the end of which the Boss was looking very beady indeed, and pointedly refrained from joining in the Amen. Chairs scraped back, and eyes down for one of the most ballsaching evenings in my long experience.

As Mother Runcie challenged me with a roguish eye to guess how much her Indian skirt had cost her in the Oxfam shop in St Albans I could hear Margaret going off the deep end about the Bishop of Durham. Was he a Communist as well as an Atheist? Snaggleteeth did his best through a mouthful of pâté to say there was no doubt truth on both sides, and it was sometimes hard to steer a middle course, as she herself must know. This really got her goat, and by the time a swarthy woman in a housecoat had put down a breadboard and a square of supermarket cheddar Runcie's ears were bright red and conversation had dried up, in common with the half bottle of fortified wine from Mauritius. Still game, however, the Archbishop's better half then proposed she should enliven the proceedings with her Moonlight Sonata on the Steinway, during which I think I must have lost consciousness as I woke to hear Margaret's not entirely convincing, 'Bravo, you *are* clever! Good Lord, is that the time? Half past nine, Denis, and I haven't even started on my Boxes!'

I dropped her back at the War Box, made an excuse about a committee meeting at the RAC, and got, I am afraid, entirely hog-whimpering. So much, I fear, for our efforts at building a bridge o'er troubled water.

A very odd message on my Ansaphone, which I assume was

Maurice. Something about MI5 bugging his phone in Deal and he could hear them at night talking to one another in the roof. One of them kept on saying 'Denis', and he always knew I was trying to trip him up. He had to turn the wireless up very loud when he was on the phone in case they made out what he was saying. As a result the message was largely inaudible. Do you think you could get your social worker friend to pay another call?

Yours under the bed,

DENIS

10 Downing Street
Whitehall

3 FEBRUARY 1989

Dear Bill,

Sorry you couldn't make it to the Major's Hands Off The Weald Rally in Sevenoaks. As you will understand, I am something of a stranger to the world of organised protest, so I kept a very low profile at the back of the hall, busying myself at the outset with opening a few bottles and expecting the place to fill with a lot of Beards and Greens in gumboots and oilskins. Judge then of my surprise to greet a big contingent from the Golf Course, most of the Major's old Regimental Association and many regulars from the Rotary.

A few large ones having been consumed, the Major called for order and began to make a speech about Old England, evoking pictures of a bygone age with hop-pickers dancing round the maypole, bearded rustics at the cottage door in smocks and more of that class of cobblers, which even I thought was a bit of the ballsaching end. He then called for the lights to be extinguished, and I was just polishing off a litre bottle of Auld Mackay's Three Month Vintage Malt when the first slide flashed up on the screen, showing the British Rail route from the Tunnel Mouth to the Metropolis. Obviously the engineers responsible weren't capable of anything more complicated than a straight line. But imagine my horror to see the Frog Conveyor Belt slicing slap through Dulwich!

'Property values', the old boy was trumpeting as he thrashed about with his pointer, 'will be halved! The noise of the trains has been compared by experts to three Concordes taking off and landing simultaneously. To demonstrate what it will be like, my friend Maurice Picarda, managing director and chief executive of Picproofing Environmental Artists in Noise Control, has devised the following Audio Simulation.' With this he pressed a clicking device to alert Maurice, who was crouching over various machines at the back of the hall, and an ear-splitting din sent the audience clapping their hands to their ears and begging Maurice to turn it off. From the Major's animated silhouette against the screen it was obvious that he too was attempting to signal the same message with his little clicker, but to no avail. The noise continued even when the lights came on, and it was obvious that Maurice was incapable of finding the correct button. Eventually the meeting broke up among scenes of some dissatisfaction.

When I got home, still at a highish altitude on the Major's firewater, I went straight into the Boss and asked what the hell she meant by it. In her passion for little Mitterand, had she considered that the value of our Nestegg next to Dulwich Golf Course had sunk to the price of a cup of tea? I had no truck with the Merry Englanders trying to stop the march of progress, but I was buggered if I was going to see all I'd saved up for since I was a barefoot boy in my grandfather's arsenic works frittered away on some damnfool scheme to flood the capital with randy Frogs.

For a few dizzy moments I thought my point had gone home as Margaret interrupted her paper work to give me a long and searching look. 'Denis,' she began quietly, 'would it not be better to discuss this calmly tomorrow morning, when you have had a chance to adjust your clothing and scrub the nicotine off your fingers?' I was considering this and whether it called for a reply, when she let fly with the gamma rays. 'How dare you? I've gone along with your preposterous idea about Dulwich because I thought I had to humour you. Retirement home, fiddlesticks! You can retire to a Home if you like, but the Lady's not for retiring! You come blubbing to me because your shoddy little property speculation has come unstuck, well let me tell you it cuts no ice with me. And now get out!'

As if to rub salt in the wound, I got back to the Den to find Boris holding the telephone. It was for me, 'a Mr Puicherda'. Maurice then came on, his sound effects now more distant, to offer me what he called 'a very fair price' for Dulwich on behalf of the Urban Blight Property Co. in which he had a controlling interest.

All in all there has been quite a deal of P.M.T. (Prime Ministerial Tension). First of all she blew her top over the Gib Report clearing the TV reptiles of any dirty tricks in denigrating Our Boys' very decent day's bag on the Rock. It turned out that the Report had been put together by one of our lot called Windlesham, which made it even worse. Mogadon Man was traced, woken up, and sent off to Halitosis Hall to denounce Windlesham as a traitor to his class who was offering comfort to the Men of Violence (Theirs) and condoning Communist Infiltration of the Media. He was then crated out to Gib to antagonise the natives with news of a fifty per cent cut in the NAAFI budget.

As if that wasn't enough, some unspeakable louse in the woodwork saw fit to leak Fattipuff Clarke's scheme for selling off the NHS, enabling that little garden gnome Robin Cook to pop up all over the place crying smelly fish. M's Secret Police have instructions to find the culprit whatever the cost in human life, but if you ask me the whole of the Civil Service is riddled with Reds and the sooner Whitehall is flogged off to IBM and Securicor the better.

You may have seen in the press following the Trade Figures that there is, I quote, 'no disagreement whatsoever between the Prime Minister and the Chancellor in the run-up to the Budget'. The angry shouting and thump of overturned furniture that you might have heard the other night when you phoned about Four Across in the *Daily Telegraph* Crossword was therefore of course a violent scene on TV and should be explained as such if you are questioned in the Merry Leper.

Yours sub Rosa,

DENIS

'... Robin Cook to pop up ... crying smelly fish ...'

10 Downing Street
Whitehall

17 FEBRUARY 1989

Dear Bill,

Yes, it is true that Maurice is in Intensive Care. It was all my fault for agreeing to let him install one of his dishes at Number 10. I'd forgotten all about it – having agreed, I gather, fairly late at night in the Club – and returned from lunch to find him at work up a ladder round the back, drilling a hole in the chimney stack with a young Pakistani of limited linguistic ability.

I was rather surprised that they had got past PC Drabble on the front door, but Maurice said they climbed over the wall from the Horseguards, telling the plainclothes man round the back that they were from MI5. There seemed no point in my intervening and I had just put my feet up on the settee for a spot of Think Tank when a terrible hammering started.

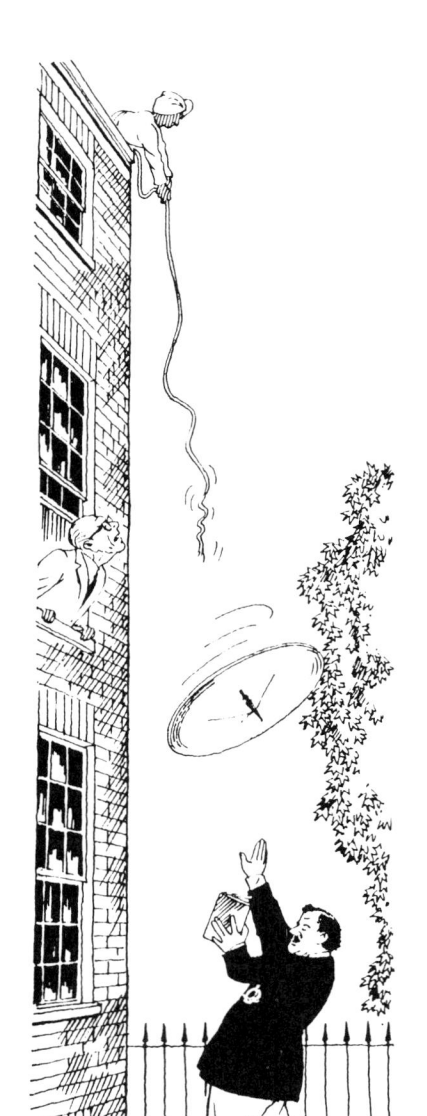

'. . . Maurice worked on the lawn below with a compass and a book of instructions in Japanese . . .'

I stuck my head out of the window to find Mr Mahut making a series of random holes in the brickwork while Maurice worked on the lawn below with a compass and a book of instructions in Japanese shouting contradictory commands up at the impassive Elephant Boy.

Eventually they got an aluminium plate about three feet across out of its plastic wrapping, Mahut let down a rope, and Maurice managed to get it attached to the end. After taking a swig, Maurice shouted 'Haul away!', steadying himself against the ladder, and the dish was about as far as the Cabinet Room, scraping the wall as it went, when a knot came undone, little Mahut clapped his hand to his turbaned head, and the dish fell, becoming lodged edgeways on in Maurice's skull. The noise of the ambulance arriving finally alerted the Boss, who had been chewing the fat with Geoffrey Howe in the front room, and while our Jungle Boy completed the installation, I was frogmarched into the Sanctum for a wigging and a half, only escaping seventeen of the best when I said I had purchased the equipment in order to see her forthcoming interview with nice Mr Munster.

Needless to say when I switched the thing on all I got was a snow-storm and a bad case of the DTs. But Boris brought in some unscrambling equipment captured from the Afghan rebels, and after a bit that ghastly cockney moron with the teeth came on in a dinner jacket singing his favourite moments from the opera. I then found none of the other channels would work and went to bed in a rage.

What of the horse-faced Edwina, you enquire. If you ask me, she deserves our sympathy. Shortly after the eggs hit the fan I was privy to a brief encounter between herself and my Little Woman, during which it was made clear to her that there might be a remote hope of her returning to the Government, so long as she 'behaved sensibly'. . . 'We don't want any more *leaking*, Mrs Currie. After all, government secrecy applies as much to eggs as to nuclear missiles.' I could see the Poor Man's Esther Rantzen bite her lip at this. 'Prime Minister, as you know, discretion is my middle name, but if I so chose I could blow the gaffe on the lot of you. Your much-vaunted reputation for competence, let us say . . .' 'Listen to me,' came my wife's baritone rejoinder, 'I have tremendous admiration for everything you have done, putting self-help for the elderly on the map, encouraging our senior citizens to do their own hernia operations, and all that very valuable work, but no one is indispensable, not even me' – here she gave the Currie woman a kindly smile – 'and unless you keep your lips sealed, absolutely sealed, for the foreseeable future, I cannot see you working your passage back, like dear Cecil. You can say you are writing a book for a large advance, say whatever you like, but not a word about your former duties.'

My friend Ridley rang me in a bit of a tizz about his water. After all the brave words about the benefits of privatisation it was now clear the whole thing was a monumental cock-up, prices were already going through the roof, perfectly plain to the punters it looked to cost an arm and a leg to wash the motor on a Sunday, couldn't I bend the old girl's ear and persuade her to think of something else to do in the evenings? It's amazing how these chaps never seem to learn about the Boss's disinclination to let go of a bone once she's got her teeth into it. If I had a fiver for every time I suppressed the phrase 'I told you so' I'd be a very rich man today.

You might say I am anyway, and I would be forced to agree. Indeed some credit on that score was pushed my way by a little woman called Dawn Rolmeova in Halitosis Hall, who said that if it hadn't been for my cheque book M. would still be washing dishes in the orphanage at Grantham. Which may well be a mild exaggeration, but it's nice to know one has a few fans even among the Smellysocks.

Re our Protest Movement I think you should tell the Major from me that one certain way of ensuring the Tunnel is completed under budget and ahead of schedule is to allow Sailorboy Ted to front the opposition to it. Incidentally, before his accident Maurice was running up some hand-bills saying 'Dulwich Says Hands Off Our Love-nests!' which should be available for distribution as soon as they let him out.

See you at the Inner Wheel,

DENIS

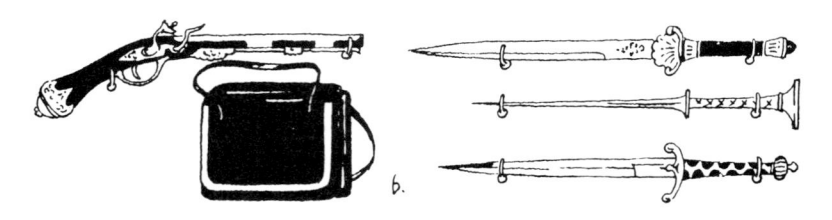

10 Downing Street
Whitehall

3 MARCH 1989

Dear Bill,

The word, according to Boris, is that he's in Pimlico though if you ask me, our lot are pretty brassed off with Master Rushdie. Until he brought out his dirty book, all was moving smoothly towards a rapprochement with the Mullahs, a lot of big deals in the pipeline, all their Lefties being rubbed out behind closed doors, even talk of Runcie's Gofer being released. Then Allahazam, they're on the streets howling for blood.

Mogadon was all for playing it softly softly, lot of money at stake in terms of overseas contracts, it would all fizzle out, Rushton could trickle off to the Canaries for a couple of weeks and everything would be tickety-boo. Howe, poor sod, then squelched his way in his brothel-creepers into the Councils of Europe where to his surprise the assembled Frogs and Krauts were all up in arms. Only by extreme deviousness did he avoid having to introduce sanctions. Worst of all, Margaret had to get up on her hind legs and hold forth about the Freedom of Speech That We All Cherish So Much In Our Democracy, which really must have stuck in her craw.

In the meantime little Solomon saw his crock of gold disappearing down the plughole, and wrote a full confession to the Ayatollah, apologising for any offence he might have given. Needless to say, this was about as welcome as a large snort to old Beardie, the scimitars were out in a flash, and Rusholme was forced to go to ground off Lupus Street with a couple of men in dirty macs to keep him company.

All this shows, in my view, what a mistake it is to kowtow to the Mosque Bros. You may remember when the bar staff at K.L. called a lightning strike on the grounds that Prosser-Cluff was forcing them to shine the bar with a furniture polish made from pork scratchings. They all swarmed out on the lawn, shouting and screaming and waving pictures of their local skypilot. P-C, who had admittedly had a few, took one look at them, grabbed the Mess fire-extinguisher and they disappeared under a bubbling mass of foam. Of course it

'... P-C ... grabbed the Mess fire-extinguisher and they disappeared under a bubbling mass of foam ...'

transpired afterwards that the pork scratchings were neither here nor there, and that Singapore Academicals were playing the Kuala Bears that afternoon at Tunku Park.

Talking of kowtowing, I got the message from the Veterans about the D of E at Bandyknees' funeral. I rang up the Palace as soon as he got back, and said that some of us were pretty cheesed off by his turning out for a War Criminal. The Pooftah on duty eventually got the old boy out of the video room, and he was still in a towering rage despite drink taken. 'Thirteen bloody hours, Thatcher! I did everything short of giving the V-sign, and all the old Changi wallahs want my bollocks for bootlaces.'

On the home front I may say there is some alarm about the polls. Ridley, as predicted, got into a terrible mess with his water, the City people came out and said there were no pickings in it for them, Kent is still understandably annoyed about ploughing up the Weald for the daily Norman Conquest come the Chunnel, Fattipuff Clarke has antagonised all the medics with his talk about DIY hospitals, so not surprisingly the Taffs gave us the bum's rush in no uncertain terms, and the ghastly old Dr Death who everyone had written off, sprang up like some randy Jack in the Box and came within a whisker of overturning one of Margaret's teenage brown-tonguers at Richmond Yorks.

If you think this will have any effect on the Boss's general world-overview you are wrong. Smarmy C. came round for a council of war, and from my position behind the Sunday Sport I was able to record the following cultural exchange. 'As you know, Margaret, I have the greatest possible admiration for Nigel, I think he has done wonders, but it has to be faced that inflation is worrying people, and so are interest rates. Given his professed readiness to seek greener pastures in the City, would it not make sense to put a new team in place?' I must have made a bit of a choking noise at this point as half a pint of electric soup went down the wrong way, but Margaret proceeded unperturbed. 'Yes, dear Cecil, I think that is exactly the area we should stress when commenting on the by-election results, a strong hand is needed on the tiller' – at this she reached out and laid her hand on his, producing a second bronchial spasm on my part.

Poor Maurice. He discharged himself from Intensive Care after his dish accident, hoping to capitalise on the Men of Kent Rally in Hyde Park on Sunday, selling Down With BR Hot Dogs at £1.99 plus VAT. But his head still being swathed in bandages he was unfortunately set upon by a group of right-wing youths who mistook him for an Arab. He has now been readmitted and is back to Square One rigged up with a drip. Would that I were too.

Allah be Merciful to Us All,

DENIS

ILS NE PASSERONT PAS!

MT

10 Downing Street
Whitehall

17 MARCH 1989

Dear Bill,

Thank you for the crate of Old Grandad which Maurice deposited with his usual discretion on the doorstep for all to see. For once however the Boss was in no mood to carp and actually accepted my offer of a large brownie to drink the health of Baby Michael (named after Mark's hero Heseltine apparently) which explained her slightly flushed appearance when she tottered out on to the steps to break the happy news to the reptiles, and also her tendency to speak of herself as 'we' – not, I assure you, a case of thinking of herself as one of the Royals but just seeing everyone including herself as more than one person. You probably know the feeling.

Entre nous, the old girl has been more than a little below par of late, a fact that has not escaped the attention of the more observant of her colleagues. That fool Ingham went and showed her an article that Munster had written in one of the blatts (in exchange for 30 pieces of silver no doubt) in which he put the boot in in his usual tactful way, suggesting that the Boss had committed a series of blunders worthy of the Smellysocks and no wonder we were getting stick at the by-election. This set her off like nobody's business. 'How dare he, after all the loyal help I have given him! He came to me half-educated, an urchin from the gutter. But I turned him into something resembling a respectable man of affairs. Now he has reverted to type.' At this she began to sob and I was forced to resort again to your generous gift to steady her nerves.

Later that evening when she had gone out to read the riot act to British Rail, old Howe shuffled round in his brothel-creepers and asked for a word in my ear. I was jolly annoyed as I had been planning to watch the Rugby on my video. However I took him into the lounge where he accepted a large one and after a good deal of beating about the bush began to do a family doctor act about how I must have seen the warning signs, outbursts of temper and depression etc. All it amounted to was that the old girl was trying to do too much at once, privatising everything in sight, making barristers redundant,

b.

'. . . seeing everyone including herself as
more than one person . . .'

the Channel Tunnel. Ten years in office was bound to take their toll, etc, etc. He and some of his more sympathetic colleagues in the Cabinet were a little worried about her and felt she would benefit from a nice long break. Why didn't I suggest a month in the Algarve so that she could re-charge her batteries? He had had this problem with Mother Howe once before when she got bogged down in her equal opportunities and it worked wonders.

I let him blether on in this vein not having the heart to tell him that any such scheme as he proposed stood a cat's chance in hell of getting off the ground. What the Mogadons of this world don't seem to grasp is that the Boss is quite incapable of putting her feet up. She might be persuaded to put her nose into the new Jeffery Archer but after about ten minutes even the spell of the master storyteller begins to wear off and she reaches compulsively for her boxes or starts ringing up Washington for the latest news.

Talking of which you may have seen that poor little Basil Bush has got off to a bad start after he tried bringing in one of his old pals called Tower, a randy old wino who could match any of us for outrageous behaviour when it comes to the wine women and song department. The Senate said they didn't want a man of his propensities with his finger on the button and voted him down. Tower has now gone off to Texas where I assume he will drink himself to death and jolly good luck to him.

Talking of winos I warned Maurice that it wouldn't do our Hands Off Kent campaign any good if sailor Ted was to be seen at the head of the protest march. To be fair to the Boss I think she had seen the red light to some extent, fearing that a few of our seats in Kent could go over to the other side. Anyway she hauled in the chief suits from British Rail and told them that they would have to run their high speed trains underground. When they asked for a bit of extra cash to make it possible she told them no. Result a big impasse with the Boss even more adamant since Ted intervened at PM's Question Time doing his elder statesman act.

On the water front it looks as if Ridley will have to carry the can. You may have seen that she publicly admitted that the whole thing was a bloody great balls-up which was widely taken to be an attack on friend Ridley. However, Ingham was told to put it about that she was in fact referring to the reptiles and the PR men in the Ministry. Ridley to his credit saw through all this bullshit not to mention the Boss's public tribute to him as the latter-day Leonardo and came round in a towering rage. 'Nobody wanted this water privatisation except you,' I heard him shouting at her, 'I always told you it was a bloody silly idea. I suggest we cut our losses and call the whole thing off.' Cue for her Lady's-not-for-turning routine. Exit Ridley five minutes later puce and shaking.

Did you see there's a plan afoot to give me some kind of gong for putting up with this caper for nigh on ten years. In view of all the latest flak I am beginning to think there may be a case for recognition of some kind. Many lesser men's livers would have put their hands up by now.
Just off to get Furniss's verdict on the Budget. Let me know your Easter plans.
Yours Grandpaternally,

DENIS V.C.
(*Very Comatose*)

10 Downing Street
Whitehall

1 APRIL 1989

Dear Bill,
Sorry you didn't make it to Scarborough for the Maximum Security Conference. Fortunately I got a p.c. from Digby Masterson who used to be in the ICI Paints Division, and was in prison once with Maurice P. We had a few rounds of drinks and if I remember correctly golf. We drank your health in the Club House before being ejected for lager loutism.
Poor Sir Custardface, not naturally at home in Yorkshire in his shantung dressing-gown and embroidered slippers, had his work cut out to think of anything new for the big speech, and he was very upset when they put his Joke Book through the scanner. When I strolled into the Leadlined Room at three a.m. the old boy was looking more than fraught, screwing a new cigarette into his holder and casting his long-lashed eyes heavenward in despair. Meanwhile Little Tinker Bell was asleep in a corner with a bag of sherbert abandoned on a table beside his head. 'There is no more important campaign to win, gentlemen,' Margaret was intoning in her persuasive baritone, 'than the war against litter. Our beautiful motorways are marred by Major Saunders' Fried Chicken Boxes and Beercans. What will the foreign visitors think come 1992?' Bell's snores might have interrupted a lesser woman,

but she persevered: 'I want a slogan, Ronald, that will catch the imagination of the motorist. None of these answers the need' – here she burrowed among a heap of handwritten suggestions – ' "Don't say Tory, Say Tidy!" We want them to say both. "Take Your Filth Home Where It Belongs" – you surely didn't write that, Ronnie?' 'That was Tim's, dear lady, you have Madison Avenue to thank for that crudity. What about "With Bag And Bin, I'm Sure We'll Win!"?' Margaret was embracing Sir Ronald for this stroke of genius when I decided to call it a day, and teetered bedwards with my nightcap.

M's main headache since she got back to civilisation was this pratt Channon. You've probably seen him on the gogglebox, red face, winning smile and very expensive suits. Doesn't know his arse from his elbow in my opinion and very much in the mould of old Fishlock's grandson who was given a backroom job at Burmah on the assumption he couldn't do any harm. (You remember the episode of the teak forest burning down, and the Company Accounts ending up in a knocking shop in Hong Kong which immediately ensued.) Margaret however has a very soft spot for him on the grounds that he's got such nice manners.

Since the Lockerbie business he's been permanently up to the eyebrows in the sewage: all kinds of warnings marked Very Urgent had found their way into his pending tray, and when the solids finally made contact with the air-conditioning he accepted an invitation to lunch at the Garrick with a crew of reptiles. He then proceeded to overimbibe the Club's notoriously treacherous old Tawny – the one that did for Havers – and told them over the gorgonzola and crackers that they'd found out who put the bomb on board, and that even as he spoke the handcuffs were being clipped into place by the Polizei. Needless to say the reptiles gulped down their megasnorts, hot-footed it to the nearest phone, and it was all front page news by teatime, with Channon saying he'd never said a blind word. The Smellysocks' chief hitman, some loutish yob called Prescott who used to be a waiter on tramp steamers, accused him of lying through his teeth when in fact, in his defence, he'd been talking out of his arse. Channon then got frogmarched into Halitosis Hall for a big set-piece debate to explain himself, the Boss holding his hand, saying he was a better man than anyone on the other side and had her undying

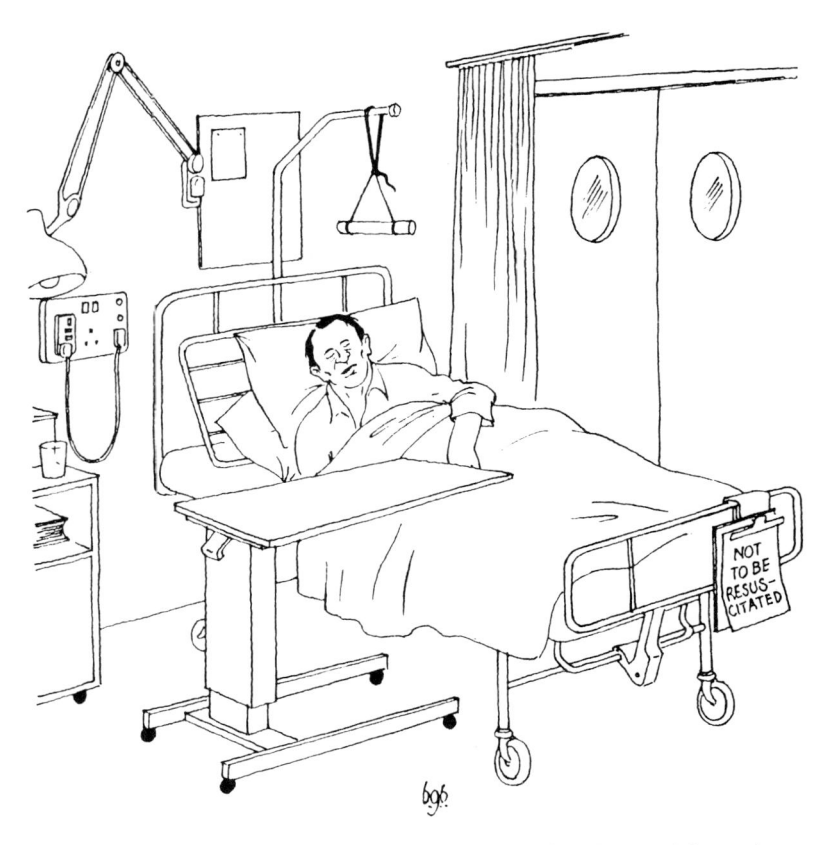

'. . . i.e. he is now in the bed next to the door with a sign
. . . saying "Not to be resuscitated" . . .'

support, i.e. he is now in the bed next to the door with a sign round his neck saying 'Not to be resuscitated'.

Did Mrs Van der Kafferbesher get you the other night? She was on to me till the wee small hours very cock-a-hoop about PWB. He'd been wheeled out of intensive care for his last cabinet meeting, all the Brothers expecting a farewell message from his trembling lips about handing on the torch to his look-alike PW Somebody Else, when blow me, in a voice that can scarcely be heard, he says he's buggered if he's going and then, as they crane nearer, under the rules of the Blood Brotherhood there's sod all they can do about it. The significance of this scene, I may say, was not lost on our own Cabinet.

Easter I fear was spent quietly at Chequers behind the razor wire. What say you to three days in the Algarve with the drinks trolley?

Your Old Easter Bunny,

DENIS

P.S. I'm glad you noted my brief trip to the US of A. As you surmise my busy schedule did not permit me, alas, to visit the Boy Mark to break a bottle of champagne over the baby's head.

10 Downing Street
Whitehall

14 APRIL 1989

Dear Bill,
I hope you got my p.c. from the Villa Kafferbesher. Don't breathe a word to a soul, but most of the time the Boss was hobnobbing with our Chocolate Chums, her better half, thinly disguised in dark glasses and a cigarette holder, was smiting the prune with Brother Boer on the other side of the wire and setting up some pretty big deals on behalf of Maurice's Pickex Nuclear Waste Business, on whose board I agreed to serve at a nominal retainer.

I am amazed at what you tell me about the Boss's Miracle Mission as reported in the British press. The cutting you sent from the *Telegraph* about the abolition of apartheid thanks to her intervention, the release of Comrade Mandela and her unscheduled lightning visit to preside over independence celebrations in Namibia went unnoticed, it has to be said, at Chateau Kafferbesher.

All we saw on TVSA, to the accompaniment of a pretty shirty commentary, was some orange-tinted film of Great White Mother engaged in multiracial intercourse at the bottom of a slit trench with that Communist dictator Ebagum, President Machete of Mozambique and a couple of coon squaddies. Even Mrs Van der K., despite my presence, gulped on her Pimm's, and Mr Van der K. actually excused himself 'to take

'... setting up some pretty big deals on behalf of Maurice's Pickex Nuclear Waste Business...'

a breath of air on the stoep', pulling the plug very noisily to indicate his displeasure.

I heard on the grapevine that she did ring PWB later to explain that it was all being done for his benefit: front-line Johnnies to be sold the line he was about to turn over a new leaf, no sanctions necessary etc, but I think he may be too far gone to have taken it in, and his only response was to invade Namibia, thus wrecking the Boss's chance of being filmed by the world's media waving her magic wand and bringing peace to the war-torn former dependency.

As if that wasn't enough, as soon as we both got back, jet-lagged and weary, and I myself was unloading my duty-free crate and putting my golfing bags in the trouser-press, little

Lord Young invited himself round for a 'chat'. 'Never mind, Denis, he won't keep me long. What is it I always say? "Other people come to me with their problems, but David comes to me with his achievements." ' At this the suited former property magnate from Finchley was ushered in by Boris looking somewhat down in the mouth. It transpired that in our absence the tall German who owns the *Observer* had brought out a mid-week comic, serialising the so-called Secret DTI Report, already several years late, on the take-over of Harrods by that Egyptian friend of Maurice's. (Do you remember a meeting very late one night at a flat in Park Lane when they gave us a lot of gold ashtrays and a list of useful contacts in Dubai?)

'Personally, Prime Minister, I feel that nothing is to be gained now by suppressing the report, and we run the risk of being made to look fools as we were over *Spycatcher*.' I could see from the glint in the proprietorial eye that this was a bad move. 'Fools, Mr Young? Who said anything about fools?' 'I only meant, Prime Minister, that my predecessor, Mr Tebbit, may have been ill-advised in accepting Mr Al Fayed's credentials at, shall we say, the face value presented by Messrs Kleinwort-Benson, and that . . .'

'Don't try to put the blame on poor Norman,' my wife rasped, 'he has suffered enough. There is no question of the report being published in our lifetime. As to Herr Rowland and his pathetic henchman Monsieur du Cann, they are plainly guilty of contempt of court. Get Mayhew on to it and see what charges can be brought against them.'

Hardly had the dust settled than a fresh blow was to fall. Do you remember that little cookie-pusher with the funny hair, Leon Brittan? After the Westland fiasco a couple of years back he agreed to stay mum in exchange for a knighthood and a free meal-ticket to the gastronomic capitals of Europe in the steps of that one with the red face who can't pronounce his 'R's. Blow me down, twenty-four months after the event, if he doesn't go on the box and put the boot in, naming M's factotum B. Ingham and her Buttons, a little pratt called Powell, for having leaked the letter that did for Tarzan.

Margaret, inevitably, was fit to be tied, and frothed at the mouth for some hours, ringing up the Palace and asking the D of E, who was the only person near the phone, whether it was possible to take his knighthood back like they did with

Piggot's gong. The old boy was very brassed off at being interrupted when he was watching a dirty video, and gave her a piece of his mind, which I am sure he will regret.

Your April Fool photograph of me and Pamella holding hands in that drinking club gave me no end of a chuckle. Isn't it amazing how people can mock up these photos nowadays to make them look so real? It completely convinced Boris, who rolled his eyes, nudged me in the ribs, and said he hoped the *Sun* didn't get hold of it. Could I ask you to destroy the negative just in case? A joke's a joke, but you can't be too careful these days.

What price some glamour pics of me and the lovely Raisa? If you ask me the whole visit was a lot of piss and wind except it did give Margaret the chance to rattle the bars of HM's cage re her forthcoming non-visit to Moscow. She now talks as if she were managing the Royals like some downmarket pop group, telling the Press they were fully booked up for months ahead but that she would pencil something in for 1994.

Yours in trepidation,

DENIS

10 Downing Street Whitehall

28 APRIL 1989

Dear Bill,

Good news from Halitosis Hall. The tall German who owns the *Observer* is being summoned to give an account of himself and has been advised to pack his toothbrush for a longish stay at the Tower. Serve the bugger right in my view for trying to drag me and Mark through the effluent on account of our close emotional relationship with the Al Fraudi Brothers.

You asked me how little Walker (last of the Wets) gets away with it, and I will tell you. As you may remember he came up the drainpipe years ago under Sailor Ted with a lot of smelly fish in his briefcase. Now he poses as Mr One Nation, the Voice of the Shires, the Old Aristocracy etc, much in the manner of that barrow-boy we had at Burma – Perkins? Thompson? some name like that – who had his coat of arms run up by the College of Heralds. Over the years he has, as you so shrewdly observed, got up the Boss's nose in no uncertain manner, as a result of which his bed has been shifted nearer and nearer the door, to the point of being actually in the corridor – i.e. the Welsh Office. His latest act of insolence was to make a speech for some Inner Wheel do, calling for a return to the bad old days of big Government handouts and pointing to the Land of Leek and Burning Cottage as an example of how priming the pump can produce gushers of Japanese money. The Boss was all for having him in at once for the death by a thousand handbags, but little Bell persuaded her to delay the day of judgement until after the by-election, pleading that Walker's speech might win over enough floating Taffs to rescue the seat. Come the next shuffle however both he and Channon, mark my words, will finally be wheeled away to the Chapel of Rest.

Mother's main concern at the moment is to be seen to be doing for the Football Hooligan what she did for General Galtieri. The big idea is that all the Skinhead Scum will in future have to apply in triplicate with details of their family tree, grandmother's religion etc, after which in the course of time they will be given a plastic dish, primed with all kinds of electronic wizardry, which when inserted into an automated turnstile costing several million pounds will allow them access to the Hamilton Academicals v. Bognor Third Round Replay match (or alternatively, be swallowed never to be seen again). The fact that every other person on earth has come out against this idea on the grounds of expense, impracticability, inconvenience to law-abiding University Lecturers with an interest in their Roots, only seems to inflame her resolve.

I mean honestly, Bill, can you imagine these cleanshaven orang-outangs flushed to the gills with electric soup and razor blades in their toecaps, queuing up politely like customers at the Tunbridge Wells Amicable Building Society waiting to put their plastic in the little slot? In the end Hurd and Co. had to organise a round robin from the Cabinet, presented by Whitelaw, as one too shell-shocked and shattered for any other damage to have any effect. Bell being keen as he is to promote the new Compassionate Caring Look, some moratorium has now been agreed.

'... *I had to call in on O'Gooley in Harley Street* ...'

All in all, back-tracking is the name of the game. I had to call in on O'Gooley in Harley Street to have my annual wee in his bottle for the benefit of the Scottish Widows, and he said that, in future, under Margaret's new measures, he'd have to think very seriously, calculator in hand, about whether the life of someone like me was worth prolonging, and whether I shouldn't be allowed to fade away in dignity on the pavement outside his premises. Apparently the entire medical profession is chewing the rug over Fattipuff Clarke, and when his cocky little side-kick Mellors came down to address the BMA Darts Club he was barracked by the sawbones and pelted with used swabs.

Their rage, I may add, is nothing compared to that of the striped trouser brigade in the funny wigs led by the Lord High Bonkers himself, Q. Hailsham. M. auditioned for years for his successor, the only qualification necessary being a readiness to bugger the other lawyers about with a view to snipping a couple of million off the Legal Aid Bill. In the end the only person she found who would go through with it was a little Wee Free Johnny called McKay, who's about as much use as a poof in a knocking shop. Result, stalemate.

Bell has been advising M. to play down the Tenth Anniversary, saying it would only remind people that the country was once governable without her, so it's business as usual and no flowers by request.

Are you coming to Maurice's Mead Tasting at Sandwich in aid of his overdraft? The Widow Flack is flying over from Portugal, so it promises to be quite an occasion.

Yours in place,

DENIS

10 Downing Street
Whitehall

12 MAY 1989

Dear Bill,

Do thank Daphne for sending up the sheaf of wild flowers to mark Margaret's millennium. Unfortunately they arrived in a rather bedraggled state and Boris threw them in the dustbin, but don't tell the Memsahib. I'm glad to say that our American cousins-in-law have now departed, leaving behind a heap of disposable nappies and jars of baby food, discarded after being put through Boris's scanner.

The whole idea of Hail to the Grannie was the brainchild of our clean-living friend Mr Bell. Given the forecast for Glamorgan, the plan was that the nation was to be 'gobsmacked' on the day preceding the poll with pictures of the proud Grandma gooing and simpering over Baby Michael whilst Grandpappy hovered about in the background trying to look sober. As you will imagine, the boat had to be pushed out in no small measure to persuade the grisly Mark to leave his used car lot in downtown Swanee, especially as we have entirely ignored the whole ghastly business since the first news of a Bun in the Oven drifted over. Yours truly had to stump up the price of two and a half Day Returns on Concorde, a thousand pounds' worth of Harrods' Vouchers from my Egyptian friend Mr Al Fayed, two tickets for a champagne-style gala evening at Raymond's Revue Bar and a down payment of two and a half thou. in used fivers. After all that you'd think the least the little bugger could do would be to summon up a smile for the photo-call. 'Give us a grin then, Dad!' cried one of the reptiles. M. was all in favour, murmuring 'Go on, darling, it's a marginal' through clenched teeth, and there you are, when the pictures come out, the son and heir glowering into the lens like a war criminal facing execution. Needless to say, Bell's little scheme proved about as much use as a rubber johnny dispenser in a nunnery. Loyal photographs dutifully appeared, Boss comparing herself to a Bengal Tiger defending its first grandcub (while its mangy old mate nodded off wearing its nose away against the bars) and surprise surprise our man limps in minus his trousers a strong seventh.

I don't know about you, but I get the feeling Dulwich may be becoming more than a pipe dream. I was in the Club the other morning, waiting for the grille to go up, with a couple of old topers sitting over by the window where they couldn't see me come in, and one said to the other, 'Ten years is enough in my opinion. I was all for the little woman when she came in to muck out, don't you know.' He trailed off a bit after this, and the other chap said, 'I feel sorry for the husband. They say the drink's got to his brain. Can't blame him. It's not a natural life.' At this I cleared my throat loudly, they both went very red in the face, and kept me in drink till lunchtime.

Poor Fatty next door got his come-uppance last Friday. Do you remember the American with the tartan suitcases, used to work upstairs with the Boss? Walters? Harrod? No matter. Anyway she's got him back. Come tincture time she hammers on the wall, bellowing for the Chancellor, and our Nige puffs in, looking very out of condition. 'Dear Nigel, of course you remember Professor Whatnot,' she said with icy composure, 'he is here to lend you a hand with the figures.' I could see that our chubby friend was pretty miffed at this. 'Don't think there's any need for that, thank you, Margaret. We seem to be ticking over quite nicely, thank you, Professor.' 'Indeed,' queried our transatlantic companion, removing his pipe, 'with inflation running at eight per cent? I envy you your sanguine

'. . . "I feel sorry for the husband. They say the drink's got to his brain . . ."'

view, Chancellor!' 'A mere blip,' riposted the Bunter of Number 11, 'we have seen it before. All the forecasts predict a soft landing.' 'Nevertheless, Nigel, the Professor here will have a desk in your office until further notice. I have asked Sir Robin Butler to arrange it' – he being the Number One Gopher and furniture remover who took over from that D.O.M. Armstrong who did a bunk with the catering lady. 'Now you listen to me for a change, Margaret. My office is cramped enough as it is. Besides, as you well know, I am allergic to pipe smoke.' There was more huffing and puffing in this vein, but at the end of the day I got the impression that the Professor would be implanted, very much on the lines of that thing they put into Maurice's backside to make him turn green every time he caught a sniff of the amber.

The only good laugh in the whole bloody Jubilee was the

appearance of Sailor Ted at the big lunch. Do you remember some story we did at school where everyone was tucking into the steak and kidney and knocking back the fancy wines when suddenly Mine Host goes pale and sees a bloke looming in through the french windows whom he knows for a dead cert he bumped off a couple of years before? I seem to remember it put a bit of a dampener on the fun and games. A very similar scene to when our blue-rinsed friend shuffled up the steps into the drawing room to offer M. his congratulations. He shook the Boss's hand very warmly while the flash-bulbs popped, but I could see the old girl's blood turning to ice. I think it was the grin that did it.

Are you still on for the Sponsored De-Bag the Bishop of Durham in aid of Maurice's overdraft? Maurice's scheme is to lob a smoke grenade during his sermon, and then for three or four of us to storm the pulpit and scissor through his braces before he knows what's hit him. I thought if we were all to get pretty hogwhimpering beforehand it could be mildly amusing.

Yours in the Cope and Mitre,

DENIS

10 Downing Street
Whitehall

26 MAY 1989

Dear Bill,

I don't know whether Maurice has rung you, but he was very incoherent when I spoke to him the other night.

As you probably know he shipped out some sample crates of his new Arden Water 'bottled from the Wishing Well at the bottom of Anne Hathaway's Cottage Garden', and the people in Brussels sent it all back saying it was solid chlorine and making him fill in a long form listing the 'analyse chimique', whatever that may mean. I happened to mention it to the Boss in a lull over breakfast and her eyes fair glowed with fire. 'This is exactly what we're up against, Denis,' she began in low gear, 'Socialists, Red Tape, strangling the efforts of the British businessman like your friend. We have not spent all these years rolling back the carpet of state control only to be buried under Monsieur Zut Alors' avalanche of left-wing regulations.' Moments later Mogadon – he of the brothel-creepers and steamed-up giglamps – shuffled in bearing an armful of post from Brussels. 'Nothing to worry your pretty head about, Margaret,' he began blandly. 'I think we can live with a token trade unionist in the Boardroom. Need someone to serve the drinks, what?' I spotted at once that this was the wrong tone to take with the Old Girl, and Krakatoa predictably lifted off. 'You see what I mean, Denis! Trade unionists in the Boardroom. Back into the filth from which we have so painfully lifted ourselves! I am surprised at you, Geoffrey, for failing to see the Wooden Horse when it is pushed through your own front door! This is Communism. Government by alien diktat. No wonder the Europeans are still gibbering in the dark ages while we stride forward into the light!'

'Ahem, aha, you may well be right,' soothed the master of diplomacy, removing a peppermint from his mouth and wrapping it in his handerkerchief, 'but of course many of these Euroregulations are very trivial. Like for instance this . . .' He slid a sheaf of papers under Margaret's nose headed 'Réglements pour les Gauloises'. 'What is this?' she shrieked. 'My French, as you know, Sir Geoffrey, is something I have no time to study.' 'You'll see that it's a very minor alteration in the wording we have to put on cigarette cartons.'

Hoping to help things forward I produced a packet of Senior Service Untipped. 'Ah yes,' mused Sir Geoffrey, looking at it through his bifocals. 'Instead of "*can* seriously damage your whatnot", it's got to say "*does* seriously etcetera etcetera." I take it we can let that go by on the nod, Prime Minister?' In a flash M. had crumpled the pack and remaining six cigarettes into a ball. 'Over my dead body. If they dictate what we can put on our cigarette packets today, what will they ask for tomorrow? Mr Scargill in my Cabinet, I expect, representing the trade unions! Mr Livingstone to take the chair?' Mogadon gave a nervous laugh. 'Oh no, of course there is no suggestion at all of anything of that kind, I assure you.' 'We shall fight them,' she rasped. 'Beginning with the wording on our cigarette packets. I will not put up my sword until Monsieur Delors and his mad sans-culottes take back every word and are seen to eat them! How dare they? How dare *you*?

'... *Tarzan has also suddenly started flying about in the treetops like a demented gibbon ...*'

My friend Cecil would not behave in this weak-kneed way, were he to be made Foreign Secretary! I can think of many more who would be happy to fill the job were I as much as to snap my fingers!'

Matters were not improved by our old sea-dog Sailor Ted who woke up and bit her in the leg on Channel Four, saying she was autocratic and dictatorial and didn't know her arse from her elbow when it came to l'Europe. Tarzan has also suddenly started flying about in the treetops like a demented gibbon, yodelling to the effect that Old Sheer Hell (namely my good wife) should shuffle off into the jungle and die so he can take control of the Wolf Cub Pack.

The other major biff in the eye for the Mem was our 'sleeper' Dr Owen who'd been doing very nicely over the years splitting the Floaters. He decided to call it a day and announced to the reptiles that he was going to hang up his code-book and invisible ink and become a rich Harley Street specialist. In the meantime Pillock's PR man Mandelbaum finally unveiled his recipe for victory '92, which seems to involve Pillock and Glenys throwing away their CND badges and trying to look as much like the late Dr Owen as possible.

This was sufficiently worrying to justify Sir Custardface being recalled from his holiday in Jutland to write a withering attack, making use of irony, sarcasm etc. Margaret read this out at a little missionary outpost manned by four practising Tories in Scotland where it went down like a lead balloon. As if this wasn't enough, she then went on the radio and denounced Matey from next door for getting us into a mess over inflation. Matey took offence and she had to ring up and apologise.

I've got some tickets from my little Gippo friend in Knightsbridge for a week chez Mother Flack in the Algarve. Any hope of Daphne letting you off the leash? Could you perhaps suggest another trip to Shrublands for a bit more slap and tickle from her Nigerian Orthopod?

Yours inscrutably,

DENIS